"BARNABAS IS HANDSOME AND CHARMING,"
DIANA SAID. "I'M GLAD HE'S HERE."

Her sister Carol eyed her coldly. "He may be your
type, but he's not mine. Why do you suppose he's
here? Because he's insane—a lunatic."

"Don't use that term. Dr. Meyer's patients *aren't*
lunatics. Barnabas *isn't* insane. He's here because he
needs help, as I do." Diana paused, frightened.

Finally Carol said, "I suppose you've forgotten the
night you stabbed Graham in one of your blackouts.
What was that, if not the act of a lunatic?"

BARNABAS, QUENTIN AND THE SCORPIO CURSE

by Marilyn Ross

PAPERBACK LIBRARY

New York

PAPERBACK LIBRARY EDITION

First Printing: November, 1970

To William David McElwee,
    Marlene Du Vall,
    and Sherry Ferguson
for their friendship!

Paperback Library is a division of Coronet Communications, Inc.
Its trademark, consisting of the words "Paperback Library"
accompanied by an open book, is registered in the United States
Patent Office. *Coronet Communications, Inc., 315 Park Avenue
South, New York, N.Y. 10010.*

CHAPTER ONE

As the large bronze sports car with its white vinyl top sped swiftly along the road fringing the cliffs and overlooking the ocean on the left, Diana Collins had her first view of Collinwood in many years. The dark, sprawling old mansion perched high on the cliffs ahead brought back a rush of memories of her girlhood. She sighed deeply as she continued to stare at the big house. Her attractive oval face looked tense. She had black hair worn in pageboy style. She had often longed to return to Maine where she'd spent so many of her summer vacations with her sister, Carol, but she'd never dreamed it would be under such bizarre circumstances as these!

So many things had happened since her carefree holidays here with a distant cousin of her father's, Elizabeth Collins Stoddard. She recalled that Elizabeth had a daughter, Carolyn, who would probably now be in her late teens. Diana was twenty-three, and she had an idea Carolyn had been nine the summer eight years ago when they had spent their last summer vacation at Collinwood.

Pain showed in Diana's lovely gray eyes as she gazed out the window of the car. Since then her life had taken so many strange twists, so many unexpected weird and tragic things had happened it was hard to think of them as anything less than a nightmare, especially because lately, a black velvet curtain had been descending on her mind, blotting out memory and allowing her to behave in an uncontrolled and frightening manner. When consciousness returned after such a spell, she was left in an abject state of fear of her acts during the periods of her blackouts. And so she had returned to Collinwood this gray October day not for a happy vacation, but for medical treatment. For whether she dared to face reality or not, whether she

5

allowed the words to cross her mind or not, the grim truth of it all remained. She was mad!

"We'll be seeing Elizabeth in a moment," her sister Carol said crisply from the wheel of the car. Blonde, excitingly lovely and eighteen months Diana's junior, her younger sister had taken over during this crisis. Carol was as coolly confident in managing the affairs of their father's estate as she was in driving this fast sports car. And she had even been willing to accompany Diana to Maine and stay with her at the private hospital while she underwent treatment for her mental illness. No sister could be more self-sacrificing than that.

Until just before her illness, Diana had gotten along well with Carol. Then there had been that unsettling incident involving Graham Weeds.

Graham was a young lawyer who had taken over their affairs after their father's tragic death in a private plane crash. Graham had also been engaged to Diana and then suddenly switched his affections to Carol. It had been a difficult situation for both girls, but Diana had attempted to give way gracefully to her younger and more vivacious sister. Only the onslaught of her madness at that time had given the crisis an ugly turn. But it was too late to worry about that now. There were so many other things to distress her.

Forcing her thoughts to one side, Diana said, "It's all so familiar!"

Carol slowed the car as they came to the driveway of Collinwood and gave her a worried glance. "You sound very strange. Are you feeling all right?"

Diana winced slightly. She knew Carol meant well with her concern for her, but if she could only be less blunt and a little kinder. But that was not her sister's nature. Sighing, she said in a small voice, "I'm all right."

"You don't sound it," Carol said suspiciously.

Diana became nervous, almost panicky. "It's just returning here again and remembering all those other good times."

Carol braked the car to a halt. "You're the sentimental one. I never cared for Collinwood all that much. I always felt angry that Dad didn't send us to some posh summer girls' camp. We were so isolated here!"

Diana frowned. "Elizabeth was always wonderful to us!"

"I don't deny that," Carol said, staring at her. "But I'd rather have been somewhere else."

Diana was about to ask her sister to make no reference to this when they saw Elizabeth. But before she could get around to saying this, the familiar figure of their relative appeared in the front doorway of the mansion.

"There's Elizabeth now!" Diana said with pleased excitement. She had always liked the attractive, dark-haired woman, and she was pleased to see that she had changed little in appearance over the years.

"Remember, we can't stay too long," Carol warned her. "We must check in at Dr. Meyer's before it's too late in the afternoon."

"I'll remember," Diana promised as they got out of the car.

Elizabeth welcomed her with a smile and a kiss. "Goodness, how you've grown," she said. And then she greeted Carol in the same way. "And so have you. You're both lovely young women and I've been remembering you as lanky-legged, awkward teenagers. Do come inside."

Diana went in first. The cool darkness of the reception hall of the old house was something she remembered well, as was the portrait of one of the Collins ancestors that hung there in a gold painted frame. The high ceilings and brooding silence of the ancient mansion had impressed her as a girl.

Elizabeth led them into the living room and waved them to places on a divan. A silver tea set and food were waiting on a tray on the table in front of them. Elizabeth sat herself down to preside over the tray.

"I wish Carolyn was here to meet you," she said. "But she's away at school in Brunswick. She'll be home for holidays, and you'll likely see her then."

"I hope so," Diana said. "She must be quite a young lady by this time."

Elizabeth smilingly agreed. "She is. And Roger is here, but he's at the plant in the village, and his son David is also away in boarding school. So I'm much alone in this big house these days."

7

Diana managed a forlorn smile. "As I remember the house from our holidays here, it's really immense. It has forty rooms, hasn't it?"

"You're always so peculiar about such things," Carol rebuked her with a scornful glance of her light-blue eyes. "Does it matter how many rooms? It's a big house."

Diana blushed. "I only said it because I remembered someone telling me the number of rooms."

Elizabeth at once came to her assistance. "You are right, Diana. The house does have exactly forty rooms." She smiled. "You both like tea, don't you?"

Carol nodded. "Yes. We mustn't stay too long. The doctor is expecting us."

Elizabeth was pouring out their tea. "Turnbridge House isn't far from here so it won't take you long when you leave. In fact, if you ever want to walk here, you can walk down the beach and save a good deal of time. It's much longer by the road." She handed them their cups.

"Is Turnbridge House as old as Collinwood?" Diana asked, anxious to make conversation that would pass the time pleasantly.

Elizabeth said, "No, but it is at least seventy years old. And of course it's a large, wooden structure with all kinds of wings and levels, the sort of old house it's easy to lose yourself in. It was empty for several years before Dr. Hugo Meyer came here and bought it for his clinic. I never dreamed Collinsport would become the headquarters for such a noted psychiatric clinic, but it has." She passed them the plates of sandwiches.

Carol asked, "How do the local people feel about having a mental hospital in the village? Do they resent it?"

Raising her eyebrows, Elizabeth said, "No. I don't think so. At least I've never heard any complaints. Many of the villagers are hardly aware of the clinic. Dr. Meyer only has a half-dozen or so patients at a time. I believe it is very difficult to be accepted for treatment there."

"Yes," Diana agreed quietly. "I'm very fortunate. I managed to get in. And he's even offered to provide another room for Carol and allow her to live there for at least a part of the time I'm a patient."

"That will be nice for you," Elizabeth said sympathetically.

8

Carol spoke up in her crisp way. "I didn't want to leave Diana alone. I'm not sure that Dr. Meyer can help her. I want to see if there is any daily improvement."

Elizabeth looked at Diana with concerned eyes. "I must say you don't look at all ill to me."

"Thank you," she said gratefully. At least she could be relieved that it didn't show.

Carol said, "Diana isn't at all well. Since Father's death she's had these blackouts. And when she comes to, she is never able to recall what's she been doing or anything else."

"Your father's tragic accident must have been a dreadful shock to both of you," Elizabeth said in a troubled voice. "Especially with your mother gone and having no other close relatives."

"It was a shocking blow," Diana said, a tremor in her voice at the memory of her father's kind face and the warm feeling of security she'd known when he was alive—a security lost to her now.

"I think that was what brought Diana's trouble to the crisis point," her sister said over her teacup. And then she added acidly, "Though you must know from your own memories of her that she was always on the nervous side."

"I didn't especially notice," Elizabeth said.

Diana gave her a faint, grateful smile. She could tell that Elizabeth felt sorry for her. She said, "I'm sure Dr. Meyer will be able to cure me."

"From all the accounts I've read of him, he's accomplished wonders in his field," Elizabeth agreed. "I'm sure you're doing right in placing yourself in his hands. I hear he has a new doctor on the staff. Someone from California, I understand."

"He has two doctors besides himself," Diana said.

"The other one would be Dr. Decker," the dark woman said. "I've met him several times. He's quite an elderly man and very German in looks and manner. I believe he came to this country after the Second World War."

Carol glanced at her wristwatch. "We'll really have to be on our way," she said. "What is Dr. Meyer like?"

"Gray, thin, and austere," Elizabeth said. "He demands strict discipline from himself, his staff, and his patients.

9

I've heard a lot of inside talk about the clinic because by a strange twist of fate another member of a distant branch of the Collins family is also a patient there."

Diana was at once excited by the news. "That seems an incredible coincidence," she said.

"In a way, it is," the older woman agreed. "But this other party has been there for several months. Perhaps you've heard of him, although I'm sure you didn't meet him when you were here. He's from England, and his name is Barnabas Collins."

Diana at once recognized the name. "Isn't that portrait in the reception hall a study of Barnabas Collins?"

Elizabeth smiled. "A painting of his ancestor, the first Barnabas Collins, who left here and founded the English branch of the family nearly two centuries ago. And would you believe it? This young man bears a remarkable resemblance to the painting."

"What's wrong with him?" Carol asked.

Elizabeth said, "For a number of years he was unable to bear daylight. He remained in his home during the daylight hours, or at least inside if he happened to be traveling or living here at the old house. Both he and his father made a number of visits to the estate."

Carol in her brash way said, "And now he's crazy?"

Elizabeth looked displeased. "Not at all. He has overcome his reluctance to appear in the daylight hours, and he now feels he needs psychiatric help for the new life open to him so he won't revert to his former state. He comes over occasionally for a meal when the doctor allows him to leave Turnbridge. He is handsome and very pleasant. Both you girls will find him charming."

"He sounds very nice," Diana said, brightening. The news had cheered her for the first time in many days.

Her younger sister looked unimpressed. "There must surely be something wrong with him, or Dr. Meyer wouldn't accept him as a patient."

"He admits to having a problem," Elizabeth said. "But like most of the other patients being treated by the doctor, he is far from insane."

Carol gave Diana a significant glance. "Graham was right when he arranged to have you come here. From what Elizabeth says, it should be an ideal place for you."

10

Elizabeth smiled and quickly changed the subject by asking Diana, "Are you still as interested in astrology as you were?"

She returned the older woman's smile. "Definitely. I've gone much deeper into the subject."

"Interesting," the dark-haired woman said. "If I remember rightly you are a Scorpio."

"Yes," Diana said. "The Scorpion's symbol is really a serpent and not a scorpion. The serpent symbolizes both wisdom and evil."

"I think astrology is all a lot of nonsense," Carol said impatiently as she set her empty cup and saucer on the coffee table. "I blame Diana's being so absorbed by it as one of the reasons for her mental trouble."

Diana had heard this too often before. Now she reproached her sister, saying, "You know that's not so."

"I know nothing of the sort," Carol said coolly.

Elizabeth spoke up again, determined, it seemed, to handle the awkward situation with tact. "I'm sure the shock of her father's death and her own health condition has had more to do with Diana's troubles than any interest she may have shown in astrology."

Carol rose. "Perhaps so," she said. "Now we really must go."

Diana felt her sister was being too abrupt and giving little thanks to Elizabeth for the hospitality she'd shown them. She told her, "It was good of you to have us here. Now I feel more like going on to Turnbridge."

"It was a pleasure to see both of you girls again. When the doctor allows, you must come and visit me. And don't be concerned about your treatments. I'm sure Dr. Meyer will do wonders for you," Elizabeth said as she saw them out to the car.

As they drove away, Carol frowned. "I was glad to get away from there. Elizabeth goes on so about nothing."

Diana was staring out the side window at the calm blue water of the ocean. "I thought she was very nice to us."

"Oh, she was all right. But it has been too many years. We don't have a thing in common any more."

"I didn't feel that."

Carol rolled her eyes. "That doesn't surprise me. We

seldom agree on anything. Maybe I shouldn't have come here. I should have let you do this on your own."

Diana felt a wave of uneasiness. "You know I want you with me," she said.

Carol sighed. "Sometimes I wonder. I have an idea you've never forgiven me for taking Graham from you. Actually, I didn't encourage him. It was his own idea."

Diana fought to keep from trembling. This was a subject she preferred to stay away from. She said, "People can't help falling in love. Graham found out he loved you rather than me. There's nothing to be done about it. Nothing to apologize for."

"But I know you're still in love with him!"

This was dangerously close to the truth. Diana gave her sister a despairing look. "I did care for Graham. Too much for my own good. But now I'm trying to forget that and consider him merely as a friend and a possible brother-in-law. It isn't easy for me yet. So I'd rather not talk about it."

"I'm sorry," Carol said. "I guess it worries me, too."

"It needn't. I want you and Graham to be happy."

They had come to a sign with the name "Turnbridge House" lettered on it, marking an opening in a stone fence. Carol expertly swung the sports car into the private roadway which wound down a hill. The roadway was flanked by trees on either side of it which gave it the shadowed feeling of a tunnel on this dark autumn afternoon. Moments later they came out to a parking area, a fairly good-sized lawn, and a great old-fashioned house of dark-stained cedar shingles with white window sashes and doors. It rose high in the air, and the large circular sun room extending out over the cliffs promised a magnificent view.

Carol drove to the parking area and left the car beside a station wagon. Then they got out and started over to the entrance of the mansion, leaving their luggage in the car to pick up later. They were both rather tense as the meeting with Dr. Meyer drew near.

Reaching the paneled white entrance door, Carol pressed the ivory bell button and then gave Diana a wise glance as they waited. "It looks isolated enough," she said.

"It does," Diana said with a tiny shudder rippling

through her. Not only was she nervous about meeting the doctor, but the brooding mansion depressed her. For no reason she could pinpoint she felt it might harbor evil beyond her understanding.

"I suppose Dr. Meyer needs a quiet spot to look after his loonies," Carol said with a look of disdain on her beautifully chiseled face. It was a remark typical of her callousness.

There was the sound of movement on the other side of the door and then it was opened by a bent, elderly man in the white jacket of a doctor. "Yes?" he enquired with a hint of guttural accent.

"I'm Carol Collins," her sister said. "And this is my sister, Diana, who is to register here as a patient."

The elderly doctor at once showed a smile revealing the shining falseness of his too-even, ill-fitting teeth. "Yes, of course," he said. "We were expecting you two young ladies." He had a narrow, thin face and his jacket and shirt seemed too large for his shrunken figure. His head was bald except for patches of short gray hairs above the ears, and his eyes were a faded blue behind thick rimless glasses. "I'm Dr. Max Decker, senior associate of Dr. Meyer," he said with noticeable pride.

"We've heard about you, Doctor," Carol said. "What should we do first? Our bags are in the car."

"I'll have one of the servants get them and take them upstairs to your rooms if you'll give me the car keys," he said. "And while this is being done you can have your first interview with Dr. Meyer. He is waiting in his office for you."

Carol gave him the car keys and told him which bags were hers and which belonged to Diana so they could be placed in the proper rooms. Then they followed him down a long hallway to the rear of the house. There on the lower floor they found Dr. Hugo Meyer in his office. The thin, gray-haired man rose from his desk to greet them. There was an air of melancholy distinction about his stern, lean features. Diana recognized him from photographs she'd seen in various publications. His unorthodox approach to mental therapy had received a lot of attention.

"Which of you two young ladies is to be my patient?" was his first question. They were at once introduced to

13

the eminent medical man by the elderly Dr. Decker, who then vanished from the book-lined office whose windows overlooked the bay.

Dr. Hugo Meyer stood staring hard at Diana. "So you feel I will be able to help you?" he asked in his slightly nasal voice.

"Yes," she said quietly.

"We had better have our first talk," he said. He gave Carol a sharp glance. "This will be a private conversation between your sister and me," he explained. "I would suggest you go on to your room and unpack. Dr. Decker will show you where it is."

Carol hesitated, her brashness leaving her as she regarded the medical man with some awe. "Perhaps my sister would prefer that I remain," she said. "I've come here to support her in any way I can."

Dr. Meyer looked bleak. "You cannot remain here under any circumstances. I have only allowed you to come here after serious consideration. It may be that I'll decide you'll have to leave in the interests of your sister's health. We shall see. Meanwhile, please go."

Diana told her. "It will be all right."

"Very well," Carol said uncertainly. "I'll be upstairs."

Dr. Meyer closed the door after her and then turning to Diana waved her to a chair placed before his desk. He moved to a position facing her and said, "I have read all the details of your case, and it interests me a good deal."

"Thank you," she said.

"These blackouts of yours. How long do they usually last?"

"Generally only a few minutes," she said, her cheeks burning. She was always embarrassed when it came to discussing this dread weakness. "But there have been times when they've gone on for nearly an hour."

"During that time you're in what might be described as a sleepwalking state?"

"I suppose that does describe my condition," she agreed in a troubled voice. "The awful part is that I do things and then have no memory of them when I come out of the spells."

He nodded grimly. "Since your father's death the attacks have gotten worse?"

14

"They didn't really begin until then," she said, her face lined with worry. "As a girl I was given to sudden fainting fits, but they didn't last more than a moment or so."

"So your history of blackouts does go back to childhood?"

"I suppose so. But those spells were very short, and they only happened when I was very upset and nervous."

Dr. Meyer had picked up a file from his desk and opened it. He was now studying some of the papers. "We can safely say that beginning with your father's fatal plane accident, these spells hit you with a new intensity?"

"Yes."

"Complicated by the loss of your fiancé to your sister?"

She was blushing furiously now. "I suppose so. But it wasn't their fault. They are both fond of me. Neither of them would want to hurt me. They just fell in love. And they still have guilt feelings about what has happened. That is probably the main reason Graham Weeds worked so hard to have you accept me for treatment and why my sister felt it her responsibility to come here with me."

The doctor gave her another of his penetrating glances. "You have no hatred for either of them because of what happened?"

In a small voice, she said, "No."

His sharp gray eyes were focused on her. "So it might be sublimated feelings of hatred and frustration which have brought you to the state you're in?"

"I don't think so," she faltered. "I hope not."

His eyes never left her. "According to the report I have here, there was an attack made on this Graham Weeds by you during one of your blackouts."

"Yes," she said faintly.

"You stabbed him when your blacked-out mind had lost some of the normal restraints! Doesn't that suggest something—that you are being torn by your resentment of what happened?"

She looked down. "I suppose so. I don't know. I can't remember any of it!"

"Yet your sister found the young lawyer on the floor bleeding from a knife wound in his side while you stood over him in a dazed state. Had she not quickly called an ambulance, he would have surely died."

"Yes! Yes!" she cried frantically. "Don't go over it, please! Don't make me think about it!"

"I'm sorry," the doctor said. "But making you think about it may be an important step in my attempting to cure you."

Diana clasped her hands over her face. "All I want to do is forget what happened and live peacefully."

"I trust you may be able to do that before long, but it will take time and treatment," the doctor said.

"Anything to be well again!"

"Exactly," Dr. Hugo Meyer said, putting down the file. "We will begin your treatments tomorrow. I understand from your file that you are a Scorpio and have a strong interest in astrology."

"Yes," she said, expecting him to disapprove.

Instead, he offered her the ghost of a smile. "I'm a believer in the stars myself. And I also happen to have been born a Scorpio."

His revelation both pleased and startled her. She had been expecting him to condemn her interest in the stars, as Carol so frequently did. Instead, he seemed ready to discuss her exciting hobby with her.

She said, "I was afraid you'd not understand."

"But I do," he assured her. "We must talk about astrology later. When I know more about the particular time of your birth and the influences bearing on you at that moment, I'll understand you better." He paused. "We have few restraints here. You'll meet the other patients in the dining room. We demand certain undertakings from you. But you'll become familiar with all those things in time. I'm not sure that your sister is going to fit in. We've never had a mere paying guest before. And we cannot keep her here if she upsets any of the others."

"That is only fair," she said, remembering that in the beginning she'd wanted Carol with her. Perhaps Carol had really made her believe that she should have some kind of company, and so she'd gone along with the unorthodox idea. Now she no longer cared. Perhaps if the truth were to be told, she would prefer that the doctor order Carol to return home.

16

"This old house is a place of legend and mystery much the same as Collinwood, with which you're familiar, I believe."

"Yes. I am."

"You'll find this house has many similarities to Collinwood though different in structure. These are the kinds of places in which you picture phantoms lurking in every corner. And yet it has proved ideal for my clinic." He nodded to indicate the interview was at an end. "Now you may go to your room. I'll see that you meet the others at dinner."

The distinguished doctor showed her to the door and told her how to get to the front of the house and the stairway leading up to her room, then left her on her own. She moved along the dark, shadowed hallway nervously wondering which floor her room would be on and whether it might be close to Carol's.

She was trying to decide what her opinion of Dr. Meyer was when suddenly out of the shadows a weird figure gradually took shape before her. A tall, broad male figure was coming toward her and she was at once filled with a chilling fear. Before her terrified eyes a bizarre face loomed closer to her. The newcomer had a shaved bald head, was youngish and not bad-looking, but his eyes were what made her tremble. There was a cruel light of madness in them.

Diana halted.

The man glared at her in the semi-darkness. Then he savagely seized her by the wrist. She drew back with a cry of fear, certain she was confronted by a lunatic, and frantic to escape his grasp!

CHAPTER TWO

"What are you doing here?" the frightening man with the shaved head demanded of her tautly.

Before she could make any reply, another figure emerged from the shadows, and a pleasant male voice with a British accent said, "One minute, Dr. Ayler. This is a new patient you're scaring!"

The words of the newcomer had an immediate and startling effect on Diana's assailant. He released her at once and wheeled around to face the other man. Diana was now able to clearly see the handsome, brown-haired man who had come to her rescue. At once she recognized the hint of melancholy in his smile and the suggestion of gauntness in his features. He resembled the portrait she'd seen so often at Collinwood. This had to be the Barnabas Collins she'd heard about from Elizabeth.

The man with the fierce, glaring eyes had given his full attention to Barnabas Collins. He snapped. "How do you know who she is?"

"Because Dr. Decker spoke to me about her and asked me to show her to her room," Barnabas said calmly. "I was on my way to meet her when I came upon you two."

"Why should Dr. Decker ask you to meet her?" the attacker inquired suspiciously.

Barnabas Collins gave Diana a reassuring look and then told the man, "It seems this young woman and I are distantly related, Dr. Ayler."

Dr. Ayler scowled. "No one told me she was arriving this afternoon. I assumed she was an intruder."

"If you'll check with Dr. Decker, he'll confirm what I've told you," was the quiet reply of the handsome man in the caped coat.

Dr. Ayler turned to her with a look of annoyance on his tanned face. "You should have told me who you were," he said.

"You gave me no chance," she reminded him.

His angry, glittering eyes bored into her. "Nonsense!" he snapped. "You behaved in a most childish fashion. The moment I came in sight, you acted as if you'd been struck dumb. You at once attracted my attention. This is a hospital for mental cases, and we have to be extremely cautious."

"I understand," she said quietly.

"I trust that you do," he said in a stiff manner. "I am Dr. Nils Ayler. We'll undoubtedly be seeing each other later, Miss—" he hesitated over her name.

"I'm Diana Collins," she said. "My sister and I just arrived."

A look of displeasure crossed his arrogant face. "Ah, yes, you are the patient who has brought her sister with her. Most unusual, Miss Collins." He glanced toward Barnabas, who had been standing quietly in the shadows. "Since Dr. Decker has turned you over to Mr. Collins I'll leave you in his hands." With a curt nod he continued on his way down the dark hall.

Diana found herself alone with the handsome Barnabas Collins. Mustering a forlorn smile, she said, "Thank you. I didn't seem to be making out very well until you came along."

The brown-haired man came up to her with a look of grim amusement. "Dr. Ayler is something of a sadist. I have an idea he knew very well what he was doing and enjoyed frightening you. The rumor is that his penchant for cruelty cost him a very lucrative medical practice in Hollywood and that is why he was forced to take this rather menial post here."

"I see," she said. "And of course you're Barnabas Collins. Elizabeth told me you'd be here."

"I've looked forward to our meeting," he told her gallantly. "I'm sure you'll find Dr. Meyer a dedicated doctor and you'll leave here in good health."

"I hope so," she said with a sigh. "Have you met my sister, Carol?"

19

"Yes. Dr. Decker introduced us on the stairway. It will be stimulating to have a guest here who isn't under treatment."

"The doctors don't appear enthusiastic over her coming."

"I wouldn't let that worry me. Speaking for the patients, I'm certain we look forward to a normal member being added to our group."

Diana smiled forlornly. "You seem completely normal to me."

He shook his head. "Don't be deceived. I'm as sick as you or anyone else here. Otherwise Dr. Meyer wouldn't have accepted me as a patient. Have you any idea of the length of his waiting list?"

"No."

"Fantastic," Barnabas Collins said. "But come along and I'll take you to your room. You must be weary and anxious to freshen up."

"I'm more tense than tired," she confessed. "This is a new experience to me, and a little frightening."

"Bound to be," her companion said expansively as they moved along the shadowed hall to the front area of the big mansion. "But there are only a few patients, and in spite of their difficulties you'll not find them hard to meet."

"I recognized you at once," she said. "You're so like the portrait of the first Barnabas Collins that hangs in the hall at Collinwood."

"I've been told that before."

"It's nice to have someone here to turn to," she said. "Even if we are so distantly related, it still leaves us with a kind of bond between us."

"I'm sure of that," Barnabas said warmly.

"I'm not positive they'll allow my sister to remain here," she told him. "But if they do send her away, at least you'll still be around."

"I expect to be a patient for several months more," he assured her.

"How long does the average treatment take here?"

Barnabas considered. "That's difficult to say. It varies with the patient. A few have come and gone since I arrived here."

"Did they leave cured?"

20

A shadow crossed over his face and they came to a halt in a large hall area from which a broad stairway led to the other floors. "Not all of them were improved by treatment. Dr. Meyer is a genius, but still a human, with human limitations."

"Of course. One shouldn't expect too much."

His deep-set eyes were fixed on her. "What is your particular problem?"

Diana at once felt shy. Her illness was something she hated discussing, but she didn't want to seem abrupt and lacking gratitude, so she told him, "From time to time I have mental blackouts. They seem to be increasing lately."

He arched an eyebrow. "Interesting."

"Terrifying!" she said bitterly.

He touched a comforting hand to her arm. "Dr. Meyer will help you."

"I hope so."

His smile was reassuring. "Yours shouldn't be a difficult case for him. And while you're here I think you'll find this old house has a strange sort of charm. It is typical of the area in that it has a number of legends relating to it and a built-in ghost."

"Oh?"

"The Lost Lady of Turnbridge," Barnabas told her. "I believe she was the daughter of the first owner. She hurled herself from the rooftop of the house because she'd been jilted by her fiancé. She's supposed to show herself in a long flowing cape and hood to those living here who will soon die. The history of the place records her appearances and suggests she's been a fairly accurate harbinger of death for many."

Diana gave a tiny shudder. "Does every one of these old Maine houses have a ghost? I remember Collinwood had several. We were thrilled as youngsters by stories of them."

"Ghosts are part of the Maine coastal tradition," Barnabas said with a twinkle in his eyes. "I take it that you've grown beyond the stage of believing in them?"

She gave him an earnest look. "Does anyone ever completely escape from a belief in the supernatural?"

"I doubt it."

"I'm sure they don't," she said. "Every now and then I have some strange experience or a feeling I can't explain. I'm sure there must be voices on the other side that call out to us and try to reach us. But only at certain times are we aware of them, and then only in a limited way."

Barnabas was listening to her attentively. "I like your attitude toward the spiritual. We will discuss it some more when you have rested."

"I'll look forward to it," she said with a small smile. "My chief hobby is astrology. Do you take any interest in the stars and the science of prediction by them?"

"I know a little about it," Barnabas said. "We must talk about sidereal time."

Diana's eyes opened wide with pleasure. "You do know something about astrology!"

"As an amateur," he said modestly.

"Few amateurs could discuss sidereal time," she said truthfully. Clocks are regulated by solar time, and it was her experience that this was the only time most people knew about. But astrologists reckoned with sidereal time, the time indicated by the stars beyond the sun. The length of a sidereal day is the time it takes a certain star to make a complete journey around to its highest point. A sidereal day, which is about four minutes shorter than a solar day, is very important in astrology.

"My sign is Leo," Barnabas said.

"And mine is Scorpio," she told him. "Our signs aren't opposed, but neither are they well-matched."

Barnabas laughed easily. "We won't worry about it. And I'm certain you'll find other Scorpios living here."

"I have already. Dr. Meyer is one."

"Really? I wasn't aware of that," he replied. "At dinner and afterward you'll have a chance to meet most of the other patients. Dr. Meyer prefers to treat us like house guests, unless one of us is having a difficult time. Then we are relegated to our own rooms so as not to disturb the others."

"I see," she said. "It's a strange way of life."

"For those of us seeking treatment it is a vast improvement over the average institution."

Diana stared up into his gaunt face. "I shouldn't ask, but what drove you here?"

There was a second's silence; then quietly he said, "A problem of adjustment. For many years I lived under a dark shadow. Now I have returned to a full and normal life, and I'm having difficulty accepting it. Can you understand that?"

Her brow furrowed. "I'm not sure. I think I do."

"I lived in a fantasy world. Now I'm facing reality. And I find it almost grim enough to make me retreat into my fantasies again," he said solemnly. "That is why I am here: to fight against a desire to retreat. Meeting you is bound to be helpful to me by giving me an added reason to continue my struggle."

She blushed. "You've already helped me."

"Good," he said with a change of manner to one of briskness. "And now I'll take you upstairs to your room. It is on the third floor, the same one as your sister's, only she is a few doors away. But it means you'll be fairly near one another."

Diana went up the stairs with him thinking how fortunate it was that he happened to be at this place while she was also undergoing treatment. He gave her a feeling of confidence she needed badly. She began to hope that this would be the start of a better life for her.

When they reached the third floor, Barnabas went along a hallway to the right and stood by the first open door. "This is your room," he said. "Your sister's room is on the opposite side of the hall two doors farther down."

"Thank you," she said. "I'll see you at dinner, won't I?"

He nodded. "Yes, but you'll be meeting a lot of the others then. It's not likely we'll have much time to talk until later."

"I'll look forward to it," she told him.

"Don't let this house or anything that happens here frighten you," he told her as he left.

Diana's room was spacious, and it had a beautiful view of the rolling fields and the woods beyond, rather than of the bay. Carol's room would be on the bay side of the old mansion. But the room, which was furnished with fine antiques, was more than she could ask for. It even had french windows which opened on a small balcony.

Diana at once began to unpack and was almost finished when Carol came into her room. Her sister had changed

23

into an attractive blue knit dress that set off her good looks. She stood over her as she knelt by the last of her suitcases, removing a few final items of clothing.

Carol said, "I had no idea you'd come upstairs. I thought you might still be with Dr. Meyer."

She got up with her arm stacked with clothes. "No. He didn't keep me long. Then Barnabas Collins came and met me and showed me up here. I believe he also met you."

"Yes," Carol said disdainfully, running a hand through her long blonde hair. "I think he's very formal and quaint."

Diana was surprised by her sister's comments, though their tastes in men seldom were similar. She moved over to the dresser and began putting her things away. "I call Barnabas handsome and charming. I'm glad he's here."

Carol was languidly gazing at herself in a full-length mirror on one of the open closet doors. She said, "He may be your type, but he's surely not mine. And why do you suppose he's here? He must be insane."

Diana put away the few items and closed the dresser drawer. "I don't think you should use that term so freely here," she protested. "Most of the people Dr. Meyer takes as patients are not lunatics, but unfortunates who have had nervous breakdowns."

Carol turned from admiring herself to offer her a cold smile. "And I suppose that is how you like to think of yourself?"

A chill of fear shot through her. "Yes. I suppose it is," Diana said with a mild defiance.

Carol smiled derisively. "It seems to me Dr. Meyer will have to make you think straight before he can hope to cure you. And if you think straight, you'll remember the night you and Graham had that awful quarrel about breaking up. When I discovered you, there was a blood-stained kitchen knife in your hand and you'd lapsed into one of your blackouts. Graham was stretched out on the floor bleeding badly. It was lucky for you it was only a flesh wound and I managed to get a doctor at once, or you might have found yourself in the hands of the police. And if that wasn't the act of a lunatic, I can't think of one!"

Diana wilted under her sister's tirade. She moved slowly to the bed and sat on the edge of it, staring down at the floor. "You needn't have gone over it again," she said quietly. "You've reminded me about it enough times before. Besides, Dr. Meyer has all the facts in his file on me. He read me an account of that incident when he interviewed me."

"It's just that I've lived in fear of what you might do ever since," Carol said with an unexpected note of sympathy in her voice. "I'm asking you not to excite yourself and to try and ward off any further blackouts here. You might do some awful thing when you're in one of them."

Diana rubbed a hand across her forehead wearily. "It's not anything I can control."

"I disagree," her sister said. "I can often tell when you're going to have such a spell. You deliberately allow yourself to slump into a melancholy state."

"That's not hard when I have you to remind me of my failings," Diana said bitterly.

Carol looked hurt. "I have tried to be a good sister to you."

Diana at once felt ashamed. "I'm sorry. I shouldn't have said that. I know you have been wonderful."

Her sister's blue eyes continued to study her. "You can't blame me for Graham turning from you to me. It was his decision. I didn't encourage him."

"I know that." She looked down at the carpet again, feeling her nervousness increase. She wished that Carol would leave her for a little so she could somehow rest and regain some composure for the ordeal of dinner and meeting the others.

"In any case, I don't consider Graham your type. He and I get along much better than you two ever did. He was kind to both of us because he was father's lawyer and that was part of his job. I think you mistook kindness for love. So eventually Graham had to be honest and disentangle himself from a wildly unsuitable alliance."

"I'll grant you that," she said in a taut voice, avoiding her sister's eyes. "I'd like to be alone for a while. I'm very nervous. I need to rest."

25

"I'll let you rest," Carol said. "But let me warn you, I can tell one of your spells is coming on."

"No!" Diana protested.

"Wait and see! And try to remember that I only came to this isolated, awful place to be near you and try and give you some extra protection!" Carol said spitefully and strode out of the bedroom and closed the door after her.

Diana stared after her for a moment. Her gray eyes blurred with tears, and she threw herself down on the bed, her dark hair spreading out over the pillow as she buried her face to muffle her sobs.

Some time later she got up and washed and dressed. When she was ready, she went to Carol's room and found it empty. Diana was frightened to go down and face everyone alone, but there was nothing else to do.

She slowly descended the two flights of stairs, clinging to the railing in an attempt to gain some solace from it. When she reached the foot of the stairs, she came upon Carol in close conversation with Dr. Nils Ayler. Seeing her, the two stopped talking and gazed at her with appraising eyes.

Carol spoke first, "Do you feel better?"

"A little," she said.

"You've met Dr. Ayler," Carol said.

"Yes," Diana said quietly.

Dr. Ayler's strange eyes studied her. "Our meeting was a chance one," he said. "I'm happy to see that you look less exhausted."

"I had a short rest," she told him.

"Rest is doubly important in mental illness," he said.

"Dr. Ayler has been telling me the most fascinating things about the work they are doing here," Carol gushed in a manner foreign to her usual cold, casual self.

"I'm sure it's interesting," she said politely.

The doctor looked at her mockingly. "Of course I have spared her some of the details. I made no mention of the spartan white cells far under the house where we can place violent cases. Nor did I speak of straitjackets, the whirlpool baths of running lukewarm water, or the padded walls. The ugly side of our therapy is perhaps best skipped over."

26

Diana felt hypnotized by his cold eyes and his callous talk. She knew that he was directing his words especially at her, attempting to plunge her into a panic before she could adjust to this new place.

"Ah, there you are, Miss Collins." It was Dr. Hugo Meyer who rescued her this time. He took her by the arm, and led her away from Carol and the young doctor. "Come along. I want you to meet some of the other patients."

They first went to a corner of the living room where Dr. Decker was standing in conversation with a somewhat overweight dark-haired young man with a round jolly face and a very attractive titian-haired girl who was terribly thin and seemed even more nervous than Diana herself.

Dr. Meyer paused to introduce her to them. "This is our new guest, Miss Diana Collins. I'd like you to meet Brian Dale and Mrs. Hope Fenway."

Diana smiled thinly. "I'm glad to meet you."

"Welcome to our friendly circle," Mrs. Fenway said in a warm voice.

The stout young man offered her a pudgy hand. "Dr. Meyer shows better taste in choosing his patients all the time," he told her with a twinkle in his eyes.

Dr. Meyer warned her, "Brian has a gift for flattery. Beware of him. Now we must go on and see the others." When they had moved a small distance away from the little circle, the doctor said, "You mustn't feel self-conscious with any of these people. They are all as sick as you."

"Thank you," she said as he guided her the length of the dimly-lighted living room toward the fireplace, where Barnabas was in conversation with a short, stocky, white-haired man with a squarish face and small eyes.

"You've already met Barnabas," Dr. Meyer said. "But I want to introduce you to Paul Miles. He was once one of America's most prominent architects."

Paul Miles regarded her with his uneasy, small eyes and said, "Of course I remember. You are the young woman whose sister has come here also. Very touching. Don't you agree, Doctor?"

Dr. Hugo Meyer shrugged. "It's an experiment. I usually refuse to have a relative near when a patient is being treated, but since Miss Collins's sister was so anxious to be with her, and accommodations are so limited in the village, I agreed she might stay here. But it is purely a temporary arrangement."

Paul Miles smiled sadly. "Such closeness between sisters is an admirable thing. My dear wife had the same relationship with her sister. They spent a great deal of time together." He sighed. "Of course they're both gone now."

Dr. Meyer glanced at him sharply. "I don't think you should burden this young lady with your sorrows," he said. "We'll leave her here in your good company, Barnabas, while I have some private words with Mr. Miles."

They moved away and Barnabas turned to her with a smile. "Now you've met just about everyone except Dawn Walsh. She's not coming down to dinner—she's having one of her bad evenings."

Diana raised her eyebrows. "You mean she's too ill to appear?"

"Yes. She has spells of severe depression. She was once a famous fashion model; then her face was disfigured in a car accident. A half-dozen plastic surgery operations restored her beauty almost completely, but by that time her mind had become more severely scarred than her face. She still sees herself as horribly mutilated."

"How awful!" Diana said. "She must be in a much worse state than any of the others."

"You mustn't jump to conclusions," he said wryly.

"But all the rest seem so normal I began to think I'm the only seriously disturbed one here," she protested.

His deep-set eyes met hers. "Take the case of our architect friend, Paul Miles, as an example," he said. "You heard how touchingly he referred to his late wife."

"Yes." She glanced toward the middle of the room where Dr. Meyer stood in earnest conversation with the architect.

"The remarkable thing is that though Paul was genuinely fond of his wife he also was her murderer."

"No!" Diana gasped.

28

"Yes. She betrayed him, and he killed her. He only recently finished serving a long prison term for his crime. He is here for treatment before attempting to function in the outside world again."

"I'd never have guessed," she said and glanced to the end of the room where Brian Dale and Hope Fenway were still talking with the stooped Dr. Decker.

Barnabas smiled faintly. "They are both products of our modern neurotic world. Brian wrote a Broadway play that was the hit of its season, then found it impossible to write another equally successful. He had always been a heavy drinker, and he wound up with suicidal tendencies. He tried to kill himself at least three times before he was willing to admit he was mentally ill and come here for treatment."

"What about Hope Fenway?" she asked, continuing to be shocked by each revelation.

"Hope is the wife of a brilliant young executive. They have everything wealth and success can offer—everything, that is, but happiness. At the crest of their good fortune Hope became obsessed with the idea her husband was in love with any pretty girl he happened to speak to. It became so bad she made ugly scenes in public places and caused him a great deal of embarrassment. Only when she became so demented she no longer cared about her children, home, or appearance did he have her come here."

"But she's so pretty herself, why should she be jealous of anyone else? And she seems well enough now," Diana wondered.

"Don't be deceived by a first meeting," Barnabas warned. "She's still a very sick girl. The first time she gets you alone, she'll start telling you sad stories about her husband having her put in here so he can give his attention to other girls."

"It's hard to believe," she said.

"The truth about people often can be shocking," Barnabas went on. "You have to steel yourself to accept it. Even the staff is not perfect. Dr. Meyer is dedicated enough, yet he sees no other methods but his own. Dr. Ayler is known to be a sadist, and dear, gentle old Dr. Decker certainly is a blameless character today, but if the rumors are true, he was one of Hitler's trusted doctors in those camps of horror during the last war in Germany."

"I'm sorry you told me," she confessed.

Barnabas gave her another of his sad smiles. "It's best you should know."

Shortly afterwards, they moved into the dining room for dinner. Diana sat between Carol and Brian Dale. The young playwright was pleasant and amusing, but she found her thoughts wandering and conversation difficult. Carol paid little attention to her, but talked almost continually with the genial Dr. Decker. It was toward the end of the meal that the tormenting headache began. She knew what it meant. Before, such headaches had always been a warning of one of her blackouts. The thought put her in a state of panic.

Somehow she managed to get through the dinner. Then as they left the table she joined Brian Dale for a few minutes' conversation. Soon, without attracting attention, she quickly excused herself and mounted the stairs to the third floor and her bedroom. Her head was throbbing with pain, and she was fighting to hold off the blackout she felt sure would follow.

Diana flung herself on her bed without bothering to turn on the lights. She lay there acutely conscious of the dreadful ache in her head. She clenched the pillow in her hands and fought to calm herself.

She had no idea how long she'd been there in the darkness before she heard the rustling movement from the other side of the room. Terror was added to her pain as she quickly lifted herself up and stared in the direction from which the sound had come. She saw a blurred figure outlined by the dim light filtering in through the french windows.

It was the figure of a woman in cape and hood. At once she recalled the legend of the Lost Lady of Turnbridge, whose cloaked figure had so many times warned residents of the old mansion of their approaching deaths. It seemed the phantom had come to her now to warn her that she too was soon to die!

CHAPTER THREE

Diana stared at the apparition with terrified eyes, not certain whether it was a product of her imagination, induced by the splitting headache, or an actual manifestation of the supernatural. The weird figure surely resembled the ghost that Barnabas had mentioned to her. Did it mean her own death was near?

The figure suddenly moved closer to her. A quavering voice said, "You are Diana Collins!"

She swallowed hard. "Yes," she answered weakly.

"I had to come to you," the phantom intoned.

"Why?"

"To welcome you. I couldn't manage meeting you downstairs," the ghostly creature went on in a fretful voice. "I was too ill, but I wanted to say hello. My name is Dawn Walsh. I'm a patient here, too."

The speech gave her a flood of relief. Though her fearful headache remained, the sheer horror the strange apparition had brought her now vanished at once. She swung around on the bed and got to her feet so that she was facing the unfortunate Dawn.

"Barnabas mentioned you," she told the girl. "I'm glad to meet you. You gave me quite a scare."

"I didn't intend to," Dawn Walsh said contritely.

"I'll turn on the lights so we can talk," Diana suggested and was about to reach for the bedside lamp.

"No!" Dawn Walsh protested in a near-scream. "No. Don't do that. I don't want you to see my face. Let me spare you my ugliness. That is why I came here to you in the dark."

"Whatever you say," Diana said at once, knowing the other girl was demented on this subject.

"The darkness is kind," she went on. "I wish the dawn would never come."

31

"You shouldn't feel that way," Diana said, trying to reason with her despite her own suffering.

"You haven't seen my face!" Dawn Walsh moaned. "I'm a gargoyle!"

"Barnabas says that isn't true!"

"Then Barnabas is a liar!" Dawn Walsh said with the certainty of madness. "It is only lately he has forsaken the dark. Until a little while ago, he was a creature of the shadows himself! Did he tell you that?"

"No," she said uneasily. "You mustn't upset yourself."

"Mustn't I?" Dawn asked with scathing sarcasm. "You are a Collins, so you must have been to Collinwood and heard its legends."

"I haven't spent any time there since my childhood," Diana said patiently. "The legends are blurred in my mind."

The phantom-like figure of the former model moved away a little in the shadows. "Surely you recall the tales of werewolves and vampires?" she demanded. "You must have heard about Quentin Collins, who could transform himself into a werewolf at will?"

Diana realized Dawn wasn't well and she should humor her. "I remember the werewolf thing vaguely."

"Quentin Collins still comes back to the village," Dawn insisted. "He still roams the grounds of Collinwood as a werewolf. I've seen him!"

"I don't care to discuss it. I'm not feeling well," Diana said, the ache in her head becoming stronger.

"Then let me tell you about Barnabas Collins, since you claim he is your close friend," Dawn said mockingly. "Barnabas until lately was a vampire—one of the living dead! Did you know that?"

"No."

"It's true," the girl in the shadows went on. "Ask him. He won't deny it. Not if he's truly your friend. That is why he is here as a patient!"

"I don't understand," she said unhappily.

"Barnabas has thrown off the vampire curse. He's attempting to adjust to becoming a normal human again, and not a ghostly creature of the night preying on young women for their blood!"

"He could never have been that!" she protested.

"He was!" the other girl taunted her. "And in the daylight he retired to his casket in the cellars of the old house at Collinwood and slept until the dusk came. That was how your fine Barnabas survived."

"You're making it up!"

"Ask him," Dawn Walsh gloated. "Ask him how many times he was told to leave Collinsport, and why."

"Barnabas is fine and charming," Diana argued, her ability to think blurred by the overwhelming headache.

"Oh, he can be that. But that is only a part of the story. Wait until he decides to turn back to his old game and sink his teeth in your pretty throat!"

"You mustn't say such wild things about him!"

"You think I'm mad!" Dawn said with a hysterical laugh.

"I know you're not well."

"I'm warning you against Barnabas Collins," she said. "You may want to thank me for it one day."

"Please go back to your own room and let me turn on the lights in here," Diana begged.

"No lights!" Dawn's voice was at a frantic pitch again. "I can't bear the lights."

"Good night," Diana said faintly, wanting to be rid of her before her own collapse.

There was a movement in the darkness as the other girl went toward the door to the hallway. Diana waited tensely for her to leave. Then Dawn Walsh paused near the door to say in a different tone, "I'm sorry. I shouldn't have said all those things. I only meant to come and welcome you."

"It's all right," she said bleakly.

"You mustn't pay any attention to what I told you about Barnabas," the girl went on unhappily. "He is a fine person."

"I know."

"I allow my own misery to goad me into wild accusations," the former model said bitterly. "If you're wise, you'll avoid me!" And with that startling indictment of herself she went on out of the room.

Diana remained standing near the foot of the bed in the darkness with her head reeling wildly. The weird things that Dawn had said about Barnabas shouldn't have worried her, but they did. She knew there was some mystery about the past of the charming Britisher, but she'd never dreamed that there was any taint of the supernatural involved.

The pain shooting through her temples was almost unbearable. She wanted to turn on the room lights and groped her way toward the wall switch, but before she reached it, her mind went blank. She remembered nothing more until she heard the wash of the waves. They sounded oddly near to her. Staring ahead, she saw that she was on a path near the cliffs and the roar of the ocean was coming to her from down below on her left. She at once halted, and a trembling engulfed her slim body.

Somehow she'd gotten out here alone in her blacked-out state. She'd been strolling along that path dangerously close to the edge of the cliffs like a sleepwalker. A step or two in the wrong direction, and she could have toppled to her death on the rocky shore below. The knowledge of her near escape left her weak and feeling ill.

Then she heard someone behind her and turned to see her sister holding a topcoat in her hands. Carol studied her grimly. "I followed you out here. I knew you were lost in one of your spells. I took this knowing you'd need it."

Still partly dazed, Diana accepted the coat and slipped it over her shoulders. Then she stood there miserably staring out at the dark ocean. "What time is it?"

"After ten," her sister said. "Most of the others have gone upstairs to their rooms."

Diana shut her eyes for a moment. "Then I must have been like this for nearly an hour."

"I can't be sure," Carol said. "I didn't notice you'd left us until I saw you coming downstairs. At that time I was talking to Dr. Ayler. I excused myself, found your coat, and followed you out here. I've been close behind you for almost a quarter-hour hoping you'd come to."

Diana turned to her. "I felt a bad headache coming on. That is why I went upstairs. I blacked out while I was up there."

"You can tell Dr. Meyer about it in the morning."

"Yes," she said with a deep sigh.

"I think this is an excellent place for you," Carol went on. "I find Dr. Ayler a charming man."

34

"I've heard he can be very cruel."

"I like him," Carol commented. "Hadn't you better go inside and get some rest? Dr. Meyer will be giving you a complete examination in the morning."

"Yes, I suppose so," she said dispiritedly and then began the walk back to Turnbridge House with Carol. They said little along the way. When they went inside, the house was silent and downstairs deserted. They climbed the stairs to the third floor and parted after saying good night.

In her own room Diana slowly prepared for bed. Her first night at the private hospital had been eventful enough, and her latest lapse made it clear she was still urgently in need of medical attention. The knowledge of her weakness shamed her.

When she was finally in bed with the lights turned out, she began thinking of the other patients. Pity for them was her immediate reaction. Of course, she felt differently about Barnabas Collins. Despite all the accusations Dawn Walsh had made against him, she found it hard to believe that he was mentally ill. His assurance and charm certainly gave no hint of inner turmoil.

All at once the night was pierced by the shrill howling of a dog in the distance. Diana jumped up nervously. Dawn Walsh had upset her with her strange references to vampires and werewolves. Her eyes wandered to the french windows with fear in them as she considered whether what she'd heard had been a dog or a phantom wolf?

Forcing herself to dismiss the thought, she lay back on her pillow and closed her eyes. The splash of the waves continued to mar the cloak of silence that had descended on the great house, but there was a hypnotic rhythm to the sound and eventually she sank into a deep sleep.

It was the first morning of her sojourn at Turnbridge House, and she was seated primly in Dr. Meyer's office. The doctor and his nurse had spent at least two hours making tests and having her fill in replies to an assortment of printed question sheets. Now she sat alone in the private office while Dr. Meyer conferred outside with his nurse. It was fortunate she'd gotten a good rest, for the examination had been thorough and trying.

The door between the offices opened, and Dr. Meyer came striding back. He sat down at his desk and gathered up her file. He gave her a sharp glance.

"I think we have all the data we need," he said.

"I've been completely frank and told you everything, even about my blackout last night."

The doctor nodded. "I appreciate that. What baffles me is the guilt you feel about your illness."

She nervously clasped her hands in her lap. "I can't help it."

"Mental illness is no more a thing to be ashamed of than physical illness," Dr. Meyer said. "Your attitude is old-fashioned, and I'm surprised by it."

Diana looked down. "I can't forget I committed a crime during one of my attacks. That if it hadn't been for my sister and the man I was engaged to, I could have been charged in court."

The doctor looked understanding. "So that is what is bothering you. I don't think you should let it. I see no danger of the pattern repeating itself unless you find yourself under new tensions. It was the death of your father and the loss of your fiancé that brought on these attacks. With proper rest and medication I think we can ease your tensions so you'll gradually have fewer and fewer of these lapses. Finally they'll leave you altogether."

"I only hope so," she said earnestly.

"I don't want you to worry," the doctor said. "Leave all that to us. And I do want you to rest. Fill your time with some hobby. Why not do some research into astrology? You mentioned it as an interest. I'm sure you'll find some books on the subject in our library. I'll depend on you to gather some information for me, since we're both under the identical sign of Scorpio."

She managed a wan smile. "I haven't forgotten. I might enjoy reading on the subject."

"Let's begin with that," Dr. Meyer said. "Try to feel you are a guest here rather than a patient."

Diana left his office with his advice still fresh in her mind. He made her recovery seem a certain and easy thing. She hoped it would be that way, but she was by no means convinced. Still, the idea of delving into astrology appealed to her and she headed at once for the library.

The room was on the same side of the big house as the doctor's office, and so its windows offered a view of the ocean. It was a large room with a huge fireplace, and its walls were lined with bookshelves from floor to ceiling. Seated at a table in the room was the young married woman she'd met the previous night, Hope Fenway. The red-haired, vivacious girl rose and greeted her with a smile on her too-thin face.

"Good morning," she said. "I'm in charge of the library as part of my treatment. Being occupied is supposed to be good for me."

"Fine," Diana smiled in return. "I have been given orders to do some research. Do you have any books on astrology?"

"Astrology?" Hope Fenway repeated doubtfully. "Let me look at the card listings." She returned to the desk and opened a metal filing box. After a moment she drew out a card. "We have a *History of Astrology* and *Astrology and Predictions*. Which do you want?"

"I'll take them both, if I may."

"Why not?" Hope found the two books on one of the higher shelves and handed them to Diana. "Do you think the stars control our fate?" she asked.

Diana stared at the two large volumes. "I'm sure there is a lot in it. But so few people really understand the science of astrology, and half-knowledge can be dangerous."

Hope gave her an odd look. "Better to place your faith in the stars than in people," she said with meaning.

Diana had noticed the change in the other girl, the odd gleam that had come into her eyes. Tactfully she said, "I've never given that any thought."

"I would if I were you," Hope said, coming close to her. "Then you won't be deceived as I was. You know my husband had me put in here against my wishes."

Diana felt trapped. "I think it's a good hospital."

The redhead was staring at her and not listening as she rattled on, "My husband didn't put me in here to be cured. He wants to drive me to insanity. He wants me kept here so he can do as he likes on the outside. All the doctors

37

are plotting with him—they're all devils! Especially that cruel one, Dr. Ayler."

She was embarrassed though she'd been warned that Hope would confide her imaginary woes to her at the first opportunity. With a placating smile, she nervously said, "I'm sure it will turn out all right. Thank you for the books."

She started to leave the room but Hope followed her. "You think I'm a lunatic, don't you?"

Diana raised her eyebrows. "I'm in no position to think anything. Remember I'm here for treatment myself."

Hope studied her bitterly. "Wait! You'll find out everything I've told you is true."

Diana left the woman standing in the doorway watching after her. It had been an unpleasant experience, and she couldn't see a series of such encounters doing anything but upsetting her more. Carol had gone off for a drive somewhere, and so she was alone. She would have liked to join her sister on the drive, but she was not supposed to leave the estate grounds for at least a week or two after her treatments were started, and then only under special conditions and with permission.

It was a pleasant, sunny morning and she decided it would be warm enough to sit outside and read if she put on a coat. She settled down on a bench in the garden and in a short time she was deep in her study of the history of astrology. The book was very good, and she felt her time was not being wasted.

She'd been reading for more than a half-hour when she heard a footstep on the gravel and looked up to see Dr. Nils Ayler standing above her with an arrogant smile on his cruel, tanned face.

"So astrology is your obsession?" he said.

She gazed up at him with combined surprise and mild annoyance. "I have a liking for it," she said, "and Dr. Meyer suggested I get some books and spend some time studying it."

"I doubt that he should encourage you," he said in his overbearing fashion.

Diana frowned. "It has nothing to do with my illness."

"You think not?"

"I'm sure of it."

"Most patients are emphatic in their denials of fixations," he observed coldly and picked up the other book which she had placed on the bench beside her and flipped its pages.

She protested, "I've never held any strong ideas about the stars' influence on us. I've always had an open mind.

" 'Mansions of the moon are a series of twenty-eight divisions of the moon's travel through the Zodiac,' " he read in a derisive tone. Then he gave her a sour smile. "No wonder your mind is addled, if you fill it with such drivel."

"That's not drivel! Astrology is a science!"

"A science that preaches teleportation! The transfer of an individual's astral body from one place to another without physical aid," the shaven-headed young man said scornfully. "You ask me to take that seriously?"

"Medicine accepts new theories every year," she reminded him.

"Don't group medicine in with that rot," he said, tossing the book back on the bench. "I say Dr. Meyer is wrong in letting you have those books, and I intend to tell him so."

Diana was thoroughly upset now. Her cheeks flamed as she told him, "I don't care what you tell him. I intend to read these until he orders me not to."

"That may not be too long," Dr. Ayler told her. "I'd say you're showing little consideration of your sister."

"What has Carol to do with it?"

"She has sacrificed her freedom to come here. She is anxious to see you cured."

Diana stood up, the book in her hand. "I don't think that is any of your business."

"I disagree," the unpleasant young doctor said. "She has discussed your case with me. After all, I am a member of the staff here."

"Dr. Meyer is my doctor," she reminded him firmly.

"So you mentioned earlier."

"You upset me, and I wish you'd leave me alone."

"It is part of my job here to observe you and talk to you. Later Dr. Meyer will ask my opinion of your case. I doubt if I'll be able to give him a positive report."

"Do what you wish," she said bitterly. "Is this a sample of the cruelty you showed your patients in Hollywood? If so, I can understand why you're no longer there!"

His face showed gray under the tan. "Who told you about Hollywood?"

"It appears you also have your weak points, Dr. Ayler!"

His expression was threatening. "Who has been maligning me?"

"I'd rather not say."

He glared at her. "This is something else I'll have to report to Dr. Meyer."

"Tell him what you like," she said, picking up her books and walking away.

She retreated to another section of the garden, leaving him standing there with a scowl on his face and his fists clenched. She sat down on another of the several wooden benches and when she glanced back saw that Dr. Max Decker had come out to discuss something with his younger colleague. The two doctors were apparently arguing, and then Dr. Ayler stalked off, his bizarre bald head held high.

Dr. Decker hesitated a moment before he slowly made his way across to where Diana was seated. "Are you quite comfortable out here?" he asked.

"Yes, thank you," she said. "Though I did have to move because of Dr. Ayler."

The old doctor frowned. "He bothered you?"

"Yes."

Dr. Decker licked his purple lips. "That is unfortunate," he said with his trace of accent. "He is a somewhat arrogant young man in spite of his talents."

"So I've noticed."

"He lacks tact, and Dr. Meyer is aware of it," the veteran doctor went on. "But competent medical help is hard to come by, these days."

"I don't mind as long as he doesn't intrude himself on me," she said. "I regard myself as solely in Dr. Meyer's care."

"And so you are," Dr. Decker agreed. "You mustn't let this bother you. I'll explain the situation to Dr. Meyer. It has been a most difficult day for us so far."

"Oh?" She studied the lined, worried face of the old man.

40

He raised a hand in a despairing gesture. "Paul Miles has suddenly become violent. It is something we didn't expect. He was his usual mild self until this morning. Then he became so unruly we had to put him down in one of the restraint cells."

The picture of a mad Paul Miles locked in one of the spartan cells in the dark underground area of the house was not a pleasant one.

"You don't usually treat violent patients, do you?" she asked.

"No," he frowned. "It sometimes happens this way in spite of screening those we allow here. Some patients occasionally become violent while undergoing treatment. If the condition doesn't correct itself in a short time, we have to turn the patient over to a regular mental institution."

"You are not equipped to handle dangerous psychotics?"

"No, Dr. Meyer does not feel that is our best area."

"So what will happen to Paul Miles?"

"If the attack does not pass, he'll be removed from here in a few days. It is too bad, but I have been noting small signs of deterioration in his condition, and I do not believe Dr. Ayler has been considerate in his treatment of him."

"That wouldn't surprise me," she said.

"So you see we have many problems here," Dr. Decker sighed. "I noticed your sister went for a drive a little while ago."

"Yes. Either to Collinwood or the village."

"Later you will be allowed to make such journeys," Dr. Decker said in an effort to comfort her. "These first days may seem difficult, but you shouldn't be discouraged."

"I'll try not to be," Diana said.

The doctor returned to the house and Diana returned to her reading. She came upon an account of Louis de Wohl which she found fascinating. He was a Hungarian astrologer who helped the British Admiralty defeat the Italian fleet in World War II. He knew Hitler's astrologers and their methods and offered his services to counteract the work of the German astrologers. Using the German

41

calculations, he suspected that the Italian fleet would be ordered out into the Mediterranean Sea at a certain time to prey on British shipping. De Wohl had the British fleet waiting for them, inflicting on the Italians a disastrous defeat in the battle of Taranto Bay.

Suddenly Diana had the feeling someone was watching her. She lifted her eyes from the book but saw no one. Then she glanced around and caught a glimpse of Barnabas Collins. He was walking toward the far end of the old house and vanished behind it almost as soon as she spotted him. The sight of the friendly Englishman made her want to talk to him.

Leaving her books on the bench, she hurried down the garden path to the place where she'd seen Barnabas vanish. It was cool and shady behind the tall old building, and at this spot the brush grew close to the foundations of the mansion. She could see no sign of Barnabas, but there was an open cellar door just ahead, so her immediate conclusion was that he'd used it to enter the cellar.

She hurried along the shaded area to the stone steps that led down to the black opening of the underground cellars. She hesitated, and it was only the conviction that Barnabas had preceded her down there that made her decide to venture into the dark place. Gingerly she went down the steps, halting again at the cellar doorway.

She could barely make out a long narrow passage ahead, and entering the gloomy place, began to grope her way slowly along it. The eeriness of the atmosphere began to make her uneasy. She halted and called out, "Barnabas!"

Her voice echoed in the cellar, but there was no reply. She became more concerned, but had ventured so far she did not want to turn and go back. She was convinced he must be somewhere down there.

All the weird things that Dawn Walsh had said about him flashed in her mind, but she dismissed them at once as too preposterous. She would accept Barnabas as she had found him. There could be nothing to fear from him.

But just the same, she was afraid. The dark underground place had suddenly assumed a sinister atmosphere. Without any particular reason, she was slipping into a panic. She had the feeling she had been silently followed into the shadowy grotto. At any moment, unseen terror might descend on her!

And then without a warning sound hostile hands seized her from behind in a vise-like grip. She just managed to scream out her fear and call to Barnabas before a rough hand was clasped over her mouth!

CHAPTER FOUR

Diana was now speechless and helpless. She struggled to free herself from her unknown attacker, but without any success. As she fought to escape, she was roughly dragged along the gloomy cave-like corridor deeper under the old house. At last they came to an area that was less dark, and before she knew what was happening, a door was flung open and she was hurled into a cell-like enclosure. She collapsed on the stone floor, sobbing as the door was slammed shut and bolted again.

Recovering enough to be aware of her surroundings, she saw that she was in some sort of locked cell with a door containing a barred opening about halfway up it. She was about to shout out to Barnabas once more when she heard heavy breathing from a dark corner of the cell. The sound struck terror in her—she was not alone!

Struggling to her feet, she backed against the wall of the cell and stared into the shadows. The breathing came to her distinctly now, though she could still not make out any figure in the darkness. Then she saw a movement, and a few seconds later a head and shoulders emerged and, finally, tiny mad eyes fixed on her with insane intensity.

"Paul Miles!" she gasped.

He mumbled something incoherently which she couldn't make out and came a few steps nearer her. He glared at her wildly. It was plain that he didn't recognize her. He was beyond recognizing anyone!

43

"Paul Miles," she repeated his name in fear-stricken tones. "Don't you remember me? I'm Diana Collins, one of the other patients."

The beady eyes never moved from her. "Louise," he murmured.

"No," she protested.

"Louise!" his voice rose, and he came a step closer.

She backed down the cell and pressed close to the door. Then she shouted for Barnabas through the barred opening, though any real hope that he might hear her was beginning to vanish.

Now the insane man, dressed in trousers and shirt open at the neck, came stumbling toward her. There was a blank expression on the broad face, but his small eyes were alive with hatred. He reached out a pudgy hand toward her.

It was a signal for her to scream once more, but this time her screams for aid were answered. She heard the bolt being slipped from the door, and a moment later it was opened and Barnabas Collins deftly whisked her from the cell and at the same time closed the door against the madman.

Paul Miles rushed to the door with a surly growling and taking hold of the bars with powerful hands, tried to force the door open again as Barnabas slipped the bolt in place. Then Barnabas quickly guided her along the corridor from the cell, leaving the madman's shouts behind them.

Diana was still sobbing hysterically. "I didn't think you'd reach me in time," she managed.

His arm was around her, and his tone was concerned. "How did you get in there?"

"Someone—I never did find out who—attacked me in the darkness and thrust me in there," she said brokenly. "I came down here because I saw you and thought you'd come here."

"I had," he said. "But I was at the other end of the cellar. At least, until I heard your screams. Then I hurried back here."

They emerged to the daylight of the cellar steps and he helped her to the ground level, then stood by solicitously as she wiped away her tears and regained some composure.

"Feeling somewhat better?" he asked.

"Yes."

"Did you get any kind of a look at your attacker?" Barnabas asked with concern.

She shook her head. "Whoever it was took care that I didn't."

"You have no clues at all to go on?"

"I didn't see anything."

"It had to be someone with a twisted mind to shove you in there with that madman."

Her eyes met his. "I agree and I think I know who it was."

He lifted his eyebrows. "You do?"

"It's only a guess," she was quick to say. "I have no proof, but I'd be willing to bet it was Dr. Nils Ayler."

"Ayler!"

"Does that surprise you?"

"In a way," he said. "Despite his many failings he *is* one of the staff. You'd hardly expect one of the doctors to do a thing like that."

"I had an argument with him only a little while ago," she admitted. "I know he dislikes me a great deal."

"Why should he?"

She shrugged. "I can't answer that. But it has been that way from the start. He and Carol seem very friendly, for what that's worth."

Barnabas said, "I have always suspected him of being a sadist. I don't think he is doing a good job here, either. But this would be a new and more alarming facet of his personality."

"He was here in the garden. It had to be him."

Barnabas gave her a searching glance. "You can hardly report him to Dr. Meyer on such a flimsy basis, can you?"

"Not likely."

"What do you propose to do about it?"

"I don't know," she said worriedly. "You can back me up in telling Dr. Meyer what happened. You rescued me."

He nodded. "Agreed. I can do that. But will that solve anything?"

Her glance was bleak. "I doubt it."

Barnabas said, "It may be that you'd find out more if you said nothing about it. Whoever made the attack is certain to be curious as to how you escaped. They might give themselves away."

"Do you think there's any chance of that?"

He considered for a moment. "I hesitate to advise you," he admitted. "Any way you look at it, you're faced with a gamble."

"I realize that," she said. "I came here to be treated, not to have my safety imperiled. It seems unfortunate to let whoever did that get off without any punishment."

"I couldn't agree more," Barnabas assured her. "But accusing Dr. Ayler will throw the place in an uproar, and I'm afraid you'll wind up not proving your case."

"Carol probably ought to hear what happened."

"Probably," he said, but he did not sound enthusiastic.

She looked up at Barnabas solemnly. "I shouldn't stay on here."

"I hope that you do. But I couldn't blame you if you decided to leave. There is a small problem. You've committed yourself to Dr. Meyer's care for a certain period of time. He may not be agreeable to your leaving."

"Not even in the face of what happened?"

"You have only your word to sustain the charge—and mine." The handsome man smiled wryly. "And let us not forget that officially we are both patients here."

She gave a tiny gasp. "You're thinking we might have to struggle against a credibility gap?"

"It's very possible," he said gravely.

She looked down the cellar steps at the dark underground place and with a tiny shudder said, "Let's get away from here. The sight of that cellar gives me the creeps now."

"Of course," he said. "I was only waiting for you to recover."

They walked away from the house and soon were close to the cliffs. Barnabas led her to a place where a path descended to the beach with its huge rocks. He carefully helped her down the rocky incline, and when they reached the comparative privacy offered there, he sought out a huge boulder to use as a seat.

Diana sat with her legs curled under her. The slight breeze from the nearby ocean rustled her dark hair, and there was a pensive look on her pretty olive-skinned face as she stared out at the wide expanse of waves.

"I still find it hard to believe that happened to me," she said.

"It was bizarre," Barnabas agreed. He was sitting beside her with a knee bent up and his other leg stretched out. He rested himself relaxedly on an elbow as he turned a concerned face to her.

Diana frowned slightly. "It had to be Dr. Ayler. He knew Paul Miles was down there and exactly how to open the cell and all the rest."

"No question of that."

"The fright I had there ruins the entire place for me. I'll never forget that cell. I don't see how I can gain any good treatment here now."

"Try and control your feelings," he advised her. "Allowing yourself to get worked up over this can only increase the strain for you, and that leads to your blackouts."

"Perhaps Carol will want me to leave," she said hopefully.

"Perhaps," Barnabas said reluctantly.

"What about you?" she asked, turning to him. "Why do you remain here in this grim place? You have the house at Collinwood. You'd be better off there."

"Collinwood offers more privacy, but I felt I needed treatment, and Dr. Meyer was the proper one to consult."

There was a hint of fear in her eyes as she told him, "Dawn Walsh came to my room last night and gave me a mad kind of greeting. And while she was there, she spoke about you."

"Indeed?" A gleam of interest showed in his brown eyes.

"Yes," she said, hesitating. "The things she told me about you weren't all pleasant."

"Really?" He sounded unconcerned.

"She brought up the old business of the legends of Collinwood—the werewolf story and the rumor that a vampire sometimes roams the estate. She claimed she had seen the werewolf."

47

"You know the poor creature is mad," Barnabas said, sitting up.

"And she suggested you had been tainted by the vampire curse and that is why you are here."

Barnabas looked at her very directly. "Does anything that insane girl said matter to you?"

"She frightened me with her weird claims," Diana admitted.

The handsome Britisher smiled wryly. "Do I suggest a vampire to you?"

"Of course not!" she protested. "I'm only telling you what she said."

He sighed. "You must adapt yourself to conditions here, and realize that you are in the company of mentally unbalanced people. Most of them are much worse off than yourself. You should also be wary of anything they say." He paused and then with slight amusement in his tone added, "You shouldn't even believe all I tell you."

"At least you're warning me," she said with a rueful smile of her own.

"I want you to leave Turnbridge House in good mental health," he said.

"If I do, a large part of the credit will be yours," she told him. "You seem to be the only friend I can count on here."

"There'll be others," he assured her. "Brian Dale is a good fellow when he's not in one of his neurotic slumps. And Dr. Meyer is a fine doctor whom you can put your trust in. So is Dr. Decker, to a minor extent."

"Which brings us back to Dr. Ayler," she said meaningfully.

"He is the weak link here."

"How much do you know about him?"

"Not enough."

"He did have a practice in Hollywood," she remembered. "You told me that. And suggested he'd lost it because of his cruel disposition."

"I heard that from Dr. Decker," Barnabas said. "But I'd like the whole story about Ayler's past. I'll have to check through my own channels."

"Does the doctor allow you to come and go as you

like?" she wanted to know, remembering that her own activities were still curtailed.

"Yes," Barnabas said. "So I can start some inquiries."

"I wish you would," she said. "No doubt you can find something in Ayler's past to warn Dr. Meyer against him. I'm sure he wouldn't keep a person like him on the staff if he knew the real truth about him."

"Meyer is dedicated and deep in his work," Barnabas warned her. "He seldom has time to dig into the past of his colleagues."

"All the better reason for your doing it."

"He may not thank me."

"I'd worry about that later," she said. "Meanwhile, I'll have to be especially careful."

"That goes without saying."

"I suppose we should be getting back," she said. "We'll be missed, and that will start more tension."

Barnabas slid from the rock and stood by her. "Be careful what you say to your sister. She may repeat it to Ayler."

Diana gave her distantly related cousin a questioning glance. "Then maybe I should change my mind and tell her nothing about the cellar?"

"I was going to suggest that," he admitted. "But I must leave it with your conscience. You should make the final decision."

Diana sighed. "I probably should keep it to myself until you've made your inquiries. She's prejudiced in Ayler's favor, and anything I say about him will only annoy her."

Barnabas was at her side as they walked toward the path leading up to the cliffs. "Especially as you can't positively identify him as having been your attacker," he said.

She gave him a rueful smile. "And I am under the cloud of being a mental patient whose word is bound to be doubted. Silence would indeed seem to be golden."

Barnabas nodded. "That is my feeling. I didn't want to unduly influence you when you first brought the subject up."

Diana allowed her eyes to lift to the top of the cliffs and she at once saw a figure standing up there watching them. She gave a tiny startled cry and at the same time squeezed Barnabas's arm.

"Look!" she said.

He glanced up quickly, and his brown eyes strained to discover who it was. As he watched, the figure suddenly turned and vanished. He said, "I think that was Brian Dale. He often takes a walk on the grounds. If it was him, you needn't worry about it."

"It gave me a scare," she said.

Barnabas smiled at her reassuringly. "You will have to brace yourself against the unexpected happening here. Otherwise you'll break under the strain, and it seems you have some enemy here, probably Ayler, who'd like to see that happen."

"And I came here expecting it to be a refuge," she said with a touch of despair.

She left Barnabas on the lawn of Turnbridge House and went inside and upstairs to her bedroom. When she got there, she discovered Carol waiting for her. Carol was standing in the middle of the room with a look of disapproval on her attractive face.

"So you're finally back," she said.

"I didn't know you'd returned from your drive," Diana ventured, sensing a resentment in her sister's manner but unable to imagine what might have caused it.

"I saw you were out with that Barnabas," Carol said coldly. "I watched you come up from the beach together, strolling along like lovers."

Diana blushed. "He's been very nice to me."

Her sister's hard blue eyes fixed on her. "You oughtn't to forget that he is a patient here. That he is mad!"

"I wouldn't call him that!" she flashed back.

Carol shrugged. "The facts speak for themselves," she said. "He is a patient here, and so are you. I'd expect you to be extremely discreet."

She fought to keep control of her anger in the face of her sister's unjust accusation. "I might say the same thing about you and Dr. Nils Ayler!"

Carol scowled. "What about Dr. Ayler?"

"He hasn't the best reputation. They say he's a sadist!"

"Who says?"

50

Diana felt her cheeks burning and knew she'd gone too far. She'd said too much and she had no desire to involve Barnabas. Lamely, she replied, "I don't remember, but I'm sure I heard it."

Carol studied her angrily. "It's my opinion you made it up because you're jealous of the kindness he's shown me. He's very nice, and I am entitled to some pleasure here. I am burying myself in this dreadful place to try and help you."

"You needn't have come, as far as I'm concerned," Diana told her.

Carol stared at her. "I won't answer that. I'll allow you to think about it. I'm sure you'll regret what you've said in due time," she said angrily as she hurried out of the room.

Diana remained there alone and feeling miserable. She already was sorry for the quarrel, or at least the minor argument, that had sprung up between her and her sister. There could really be no question but that Carol was trying to help her. Yet there had always been a kind of antagonism between them, whether they liked it or not. She and Carol were very different in temperament and so often clashed.

Her illness had made her more vulnerable to Carol's coldness, but she could only hope for a recovery that would free them both from a relationship that wasn't happy. Each of them would do better on her own, she was certain of that. Typical of their attitudes and capacities for friendships was her own attraction to Barnabas Collins and Carol's immediate liking for Dr. Nils Ayler. Neither could approve of the other's choice.

In mid-afternoon Dr. Decker came to her room with several bottles of medications and sat for some time explaining how she should take them. The old man was kindly in his manner, and she felt that he was very sincere. It seemed hardly believable that this mild, frail doctor could have been one of Hitler's medical men during the horrifying days of the concentration camps.

She listened to his instructions carefully and when he'd finished, she asked, "How is Paul Miles?"

He looked embarrassed. "I have given him an injection of a powerful sedative and he has responded very well. I hope if we are able to calm him for a sufficient time, he may come around to himself."

"I see," she said, thinking of the moments of terror she'd known in the cell with the madman, but she didn't dare confide in the old doctor. "You feel he will be safe to mingle with the rest of us if he gets through this crisis?"

"Undoubtedly," the veteran doctor said. "If he doesn't respond, we will know the condition could become permanent. Then we'll be forced to send him away. But until then every effort will be made to cure him."

She walked him to the door. "I understand that you practiced in Germany before coming to America," she said.

A tiny shadow of apprehension crossed the lined face of the bald old man. "That is true," he admitted.

"Were you forced to flee your country before the war? So many fine talents found themselves with no choice but to do that."

He hesitated and then finally said, "No, I did not leave until after the war."

Diana heard his uneasy explanation with deep interest. So he had been in Germany during the Hitler regime, which meant he must have endorsed the policies of that dark era! She said, "Then you must have experienced some very grim times."

He avoided looking at her directly. "They were sad days, Miss Collins," he said quietly.

"Extremely difficult for doctors, I'm told," she said, trying to lead him into some further discussion of his role then.

"They were. It is true," he said quietly and then with a quick nod left her. There was a furtive quality in his retreat and lack of interest in carrying on the discussion that made her feel positive Barnabas had been right in indicting him as one of the doctors who had contributed to Hitler's reign of terror.

She followed his instructions in taking the various pills and by the evening she felt much more relaxed. She noted that Carol and Dr. Nils Ayler were as friendly as ever and wondered about this. Neither Barnabas nor Paul Miles

52

was present for dinner. She knew that Paul was confined to a cell below but had no idea where Barnabas might be. Dawn Walsh had presented herself at the table, and for the first time Diana saw the former beauty. As Barnabas had claimed, there were only minor scars on the even-featured face of the model to show that she'd been injured and had had plastic surgery. Yet, her attitude revealed that she felt she was still noticeably disfigured.

After dinner Diana drifted off to a corner with Brian Dale. As Barnabas had predicted, she found the young man friendly and intelligent. They stood by one of the french windows in the living room. This particular window overlooked the bay. It had been a fairly warm afternoon, and now with evening, fog was rushing in to cloak the old house in a swirling, gray mist.

Brian showed a smile on his round, pleasant face. "The fog gives the place a ghostly touch, doesn't it?"

She glanced out. "I suppose it does. I hadn't thought about it."

"When you've been here as long as I have, you take an interest in every small detail. Even the weather becomes important to you. And every minor change in it."

Diana studied the playwright. "What are you doing in a place like this?"

He was still smiling, but his eyes had a tragic look. "I have an idea the world is a rotten place, and I keep trying to kill myself."

She reacted incredulously. "I would put you down as an optimist," she said. "You certainly look like one. And haven't you had a successful writing career? I understand you wrote one of the all-time Broadway hits."

"That's another story. Nothing else I've written has ever made the grade."

"Wasn't that one big success enough?" she wanted to know.

"It paid me well enough," he said. "But I'd like acceptance of my new work."

"That might come in time. I wouldn't think you had any reason for despondency or self-destruction."

He looked at her with sour amusement. "You sound exactly like Dr. Meyer. He claims all I have to do is

53

change my thinking and I can walk out of here a healthy person."

"I agree," she said.

"You make it seem too easy," was his reply. "The grapevine has it that you've a habit of blacking out now and then, and sometimes you wander and do mad things during your attacks."

His frank description of her illness made her blush. "I had no idea there was that kind of gossip among the patients," she said.

"Sure. Gives us something else to do. So now I'll ask you, why the blackouts? What makes them happen?"

"Dr. Meyer says too much tension. That's what he's treating me for."

"Dr. Meyer usually knows," Brian Dale assured her. "I also hear you've a great interest in astrology, and you were born under the sign of Scorpio."

She laughed. "You've got all the data."

He gave her a sharp glance. "Do you think the stars can tell our future?"

"Yes."

"I wish you'd work on mine," he said. "I'm a Pisces."

"I'll need more than that," she told him. "I'll have to have the day and hour of your birth, and a lot of other things."

"Great," he said. "It will be something for us to do."

"I wonder where Barnabas is," she said.

He gave her an interested look. "He's gone to Collinwood—left before dinner. The doctor allows him to leave whenever he likes. It will probably be late before he returns. It's a pretty long walk over there by road."

"Does he go there often?"

"Fairly often," Brian Dale said with a wise look on his young face. "From what I've heard, Collinwood is a strange old house. It has attractions for him. He is interested in the supernatural, and it's filled with ghosts."

"So they've told me."

"You like Barnabas pretty well, don't you?"

She smiled. "He's a charming man. He's also a distant relative of mine."

"Almost all the females here think he's something

54

special," Brian said with resignation. "The rest of us don't impress them at all."

"When do you expect him back?" she asked. With the coming of this fog-shrouded night she was suddenly nervous and anxious for Barnabas to return.

"The doctor likes all of us back here by ten at the latest," Brian said. "He's strict about that."

Soon after, Diana excused herself from the company of the playwright and talked with Hope Fenway for a while. She found the redhead in a more confused state than ever. Taking her aside, the girl confided in her, "My husband isn't satisfied with locking me in this place—he also wants to get rid of me permanently."

Diana was embarrassed by this confidence and said, "I'm sure you must be wrong."

"No," Hope said with finality. "He has this plot to do away with me. My life isn't worth anything at all. Wait and see." With this grim warning, she left.

Diana made her way to the library and looked through the shelves on her own. She hoped to find some other books on astrology, but there were none. She did locate a book on the occult and predictions and settled down in one of the comfortable chairs with it. She read for about an hour and then went back to the living room.

Dr. Decker was there, seated in a chair near the doorway, reading a newspaper. He glanced up and greeted her as she appeared, and she asked him, "Has Barnabas Collins returned yet?"

"No," the doctor said, "but he should arrive at any minute, since it is near ten."

Diana excused herself, and went back out to the hallway. Thinking she might have a chance to talk to Barnabas before he entered the house, she let herself out the front door and stood on the fog-ridden steps for a moment. It was cool and damp, and she shivered a little. Straining to see if there was someone coming along the road, she finally caught a sign of a movement. Somebody was walking along the highway toward the drive. Sure that it was Barnabas, she left the steps and went hurriedly to greet him.

She was a good distance from the house, and the figure in the fog was still blurred. Then all at once it vanished. She halted and stared into the heavy gray mist in confusion. She couldn't believe what had happened. The eerie twist of events sent a stab of fear through her as she strained to penetrate the thick fog.

She was about to turn and retrace her steps to Turnbridge House when there was suddenly a low snarling from behind her. She wheeled around and her startled eyes were presented with a terrifying sight. Crouching low in the grass was a wolf-like creature with fearsome fangs and burning amber eyes. The beast was ready to pounce on her!

CHAPTER FIVE

Diana fell back a few paces and let out a frightened cry. The weird grayish-yellow creature went on snarling and preparing to attack. Its cavernous mouth was open so that its huge fangs showed, and the slavering from its lips indicated a madness. The great wiry body was poised to spring at her. She lifted her hands in a forlorn hope to protect herself. The distant orange of the lighted windows of Turnbridge House seemed far away.

Then the thing sprang at her and she felt its hot, fetid breath as she fell backward. Panic-stricken screams came from her lips as she sprawled on the wet grass with the angry beast over her. At once she felt faint. The tension had been too great, and another of her spells suddenly hit her. Reality was being blotted out.

When she opened her eyes, there was darkness around her, but it was not the damp darkness of the outside. It took her another minute to know that she was in her own bedroom and on her bed. She made no attempt to move but lay there staring up into the shadows and trying to remember. It slowly came back to her. She had been outside ready to greet Barnabas when a strange, threatening wolf-like creature had literally materialized out of the fog.

The werewolf! The Werewolf of Collinwood! She had finally seen it! The memory of the snarling monster was very vivid in her mind. How had she escaped it and safely reached her room? The last thing she recalled was the mad thing leaping toward her. Yet here she was in her own bedroom, unharmed. She had lapsed into one of her blackouts, there was no question of that. But what had happened afterward?

Raising herself on an elbow, she glanced at the luminous dial of her wristwatch. It was almost midnight. She must have been in a blank state for close to two hours. What had happened during that time?

Her head was aching, and she was very confused. Slowly, she got up from the bed and turned on the room lights. Then she stood there trying to collect her scattered thoughts. Foremost in her mind was the memory of that snarling monster. Her dress was wet, as if she'd been unconscious on the grass for some time. The agony of knowing that once again her mind had closed to reality was sickening in itself.

Then there came a quiet knocking on her door. With a sigh she slowly crossed over and opened it. Carol was standing outside in a dressing gown looking pale and troubled. Her sister at once came into the room and closed the door after her. Then she studied her with fear in her blue eyes.

"Where were you?" she demanded, facing her.

Diana swallowed hard. "What do you mean?"

Her sister's tone was tense. "You know what I mean. I was in here a short time ago, and you weren't here. I've been frantic ever since!"

"How long ago?" she asked.

"Maybe a half-hour or a little less," Carol declared, her manner angry. "Where were you? You're a sight! Your clothes are wet, and your hair is damp and plastered about your head!"

Feeling as if she might faint, Diana pressed a hand to her temple. "I don't know where I was. I had a fainting spell."

"Another blackout!" her sister hurled it at her.

"I suppose so," she said weakly.

"You must have been out in the fog to be in that state!"

Diana felt she might as well confess. She said, "I went out on the steps to meet Barnabas. He went somewhere for the evening . . . to Collinwood, I think."

"Barnabas again!" her sister said sharply.

"I thought I saw him," she went on. "And then he vanished and I heard an eerie snarling from behind me. I turned and it was a monstrous wolf-like thing."

Carol stared at her with disbelief. "What kind of a story are you trying to make me swallow?"

"I'm telling you exactly what happened," she said plaintively.

Carol came close to her, the pretty face hard. "Are you starting to have delusions, as well as blackouts?"

"No! I saw this ugly animal. I don't know whether it was some huge stray dog or the werewolf they say haunts this district."

"A werewolf!" Carol snapped with contempt. "Surely you can do better than that. You moon around all hours of the night waiting for that Barnabas and then take one of your spells. That's bad enough, without your making up stories as a cover!"

"I'm not making anything up," she protested. "I saw this snarling animal."

Carol eyed her disdainfully. "And then what?"

"I started to scream and I backed up." She paused. "Then I had a blackout."

"And?"

"I don't remember anything until a few minutes ago when I came to in here," Diana said forlornly. She slumped down in a chair near where her sister was standing.

"Where were you in the meantime, and what did you do?" Carol wanted to know.

She gave her a despairing look. "I wish I could tell you."

"I think it's important that you try and remember," her sister said.

Diana felt the same way. Above all else she wanted to know why she'd been spared by that nightmare monster and how she'd managed to get safely into the house and to her own bed. Had Barnabas appeared after all and come to her rescue? It was a comforting thought, but she had no means of knowing whether it was true.

She said, "Maybe I did see Barnabas. Maybe he was the one who saved me."

"I doubt that very much," her sister said.

Diana bent her head and closed her eyes. "Then I don't know," she said in a near sob.

Carol bent close to her and in a tense, low voice said, "You're getting worse! You know that! You can't go on this way!"

She moaned. "Dr. Meyer will help me!"

"I doubt if he'll even allow you to remain here, if you keep throwing yourself at Barnabas. You had no right to be out on this dark, foggy night looking for him!"

"I only went a short distance from the front door!"

"You were wrong in doing even that," Carol said. "Now it's hard to say what else you did."

"Probably nothing," Diana said brokenly. "I think Barnabas found me in a faint and carried me up here."

"That's only wishful thinking!"

"I mean it!"

"You know what happened once before!" Carol warned her. "When I came into the room that night, you were standing over Graham with a knife in your hand."

"I have never done anything like that since!" Diana protested.

"Once was sufficient," her sister said sternly. "Graham will be coming to visit us in a few days. What do you think he'll say when I tell him you're still having these spells?"

"That is why I was sent here!"

"You were sent here for treatment and to obey the rules," Carol said. "You are misbehaving. Trying to impress someone who is probably as mentally sick as you."

"He's not!"

"I won't even argue that," she said. "I only know you had no right to leave this house in the darkness and expose yourself to a situation that induced another of your spells."

"I didn't do it willfully," Diana protested. "It just sort of happened!"

Carol showed her no pity. "It had better not happen again." She turned, as if heading for the door, then stopped suddenly and stood staring at the dresser. "What's that?" she asked in a startled voice.

Diana got to her feet. "What?"

Carol had gone pale. She seemed to be stricken. Raising a hand, she pointed to the dresser. "Over there!"

Diana glanced in the direction her sister had pointed, and a shadow of horror crossed her own face. She saw a knife on the dresser top! A knife that had no business being there—and had not been there before.

"Well?" Carol hadn't moved.

"I don't know," she faltered. She forced herself to go over to the dresser to examine the knife, but when she came close to it, she halted in horror. Both the blade and handle of the ordinary kitchen knife were dark and sticky with blood!

Carol had followed her, and now she gave a tiny gasp. "Again!"

Diana wheeled on her with staring, frightened eyes. "What do you mean?"

Carol studied her with alarm. "You know very well what I mean. You must have brought that knife back here! Who did you use it on during your blackout?"

"No one! I don't know anything about it!"

"Don't lie to me," Carol said fiercely, seizing her by the arm. "You had to be using it, or it wouldn't be here now!"

"I don't remember anything!" she protested, near tears.

"That's what you said before," Carol reminded her. "Who did you attack in your madness this time? Was it Barnabas?"

She shook her head. "No. I couldn't have attacked anyone!"

"How do you know?"

Diana couldn't answer that. She bent her head and prayed that she might remember, but that interlude was a blank in her mind.

"You don't know!" Carol told her. "What have you done this time?"

She raised her eyes. "Nothing," she said in despair.

Carol looked wan and ill. "I wish I could believe it."

Diana turned her back on the dresser and the knife. "What will we do?"

"That can't stay here!"

"Dr. Meyer should be told about it," Diana suggested.

"That would be the final straw," Carol told her. "For the time being, we don't want you linked with this knife at all. You may have done some awful thing—even killed someone."

"Don't say that," she begged of her sister.

Carol was stern. "We have to consider the possibilities. During your blackouts you're not responsible."

"All the more reason for reporting to Dr. Meyer that I had such a spell," she insisted. She knew Carol was trying to be helpful, but she was not sure her sister knew how to handle the situation properly.

The blonde girl seemed to have other ideas. "Once you've confessed to Dr. Meyer, you're as good as in the hands of the police. He can't help you hide a crime."

"But I don't think there was any crime!"

"Let's make sure first," Carol warned her. Taking a hankie from her pocket, she gingerly stepped over to the dresser and picked up the blood-stained knife with the hankie. "We have to get rid of this. It can't be found in your bedroom."

"What are you going to do?"

"I'm not sure. I'll get rid of it somehow," Carol said, her pale face showing an expression of revulsion. "You go to bed and say nothing."

"But if we do this, we'll be covering up a possible crime," Diana protested.

"And likely one committed by you," was Carol's harsh reply. "You had best let me take care of this."

"How?"

"I haven't made up my mind yet," her sister said. "Let me decide."

"If I found Barnabas and told him what had happened, he might be able to advise me," Diana suggested.

"Leave Barnabas out of it!" Carol said. "It was your running after him that got you in all this trouble."

With that, Carol left the room carrying the grisly weapon. Diana stood trembling as the door closed, wondering what awful thing she had done. What would happen

61

to her now? How could she hope to sleep, with this tormenting her?

Then she remembered the tablets Dr. Decker had brought her. There were some sleeping pills among them, and there could be no question that she had need of them at this moment. In panic she rushed to the bathroom medicine cabinet and eagerly searched out the pills. When she found them, she took two, which was the maximum dosage recommended. Then she began preparing for bed, still shattered by the discovery of the knife.

The sleeping pills worked and she fell into a deep sleep almost immediately. Only when she was roughly shaken by someone did she awake. Opening her eyes in a dull fashion, she found herself staring up at the shaven-headed Dr. Nils Ayler. His cruel face showed annoyance.

"What does it take to wake you up?" the young doctor demanded.

"I'm sorry," she said. "I took some pills. What time is it?"

"Mid-morning," he told her sternly. "You should have been down for an appointment with Dr. Meyer an hour ago."

She was still in a daze. "I overslept."

His expression was sarcastic. "That's obvious. You'll do well to get up and dressed at once. The clinic is in a state this morning. Mrs. Hope Fenway has vanished."

"Vanished?" she echoed stupidly.

"That's what I said," he snapped. "And if that wasn't bad enough, you picked today to drug yourself with pills. We thought something might have happened to you, as well."

"I'm all right," she said in a weak voice.

He remained at her bedside a moment longer to say, "I'll inform Dr. Meyer that you'll be downstairs within the half-hour."

"Yes," she agreed.

He went out and she sat up in bed. Memory was returning to her, and she recalled the fantastic series of events of the previous night. Perhaps the unhappy Hope Fenway had fallen victim to that monster of an animal which had stalked her. She couldn't erase her encounter with the eerie creature from her mind. If only she hadn't slipped into that blackout!

But she had, and no memory of the events following the terrifying encounter remained. How had she escaped? When had she returned to her room? And had she managed it on her own or been assisted by Barnabas? Most troublesome of all, what had that blood-stained knife been doing on her dresser, and where had it come from?

Somehow she washed and dressed. She was apprehensive about making her way downstairs, but she had to do it. She first went to Carol's room to ask her sister what she'd done with the macabre weapon. Her sister wasn't there, so she went on downstairs.

She met Brian Dale standing at the foot of the stairway. Diana at once saw that he was in a troubled state.

"What is the news about Hope Fenway?"

He sighed. "They've found her. Poor soul! She's at rest at last."

Diana felt a rush of sorrow. "She's dead?"

"Yes." The young man stared at her bleakly. "Murdered."

"Murdered!"

"They found her near the cliffs. She'd been stabbed several times, and whoever did it used a lipstick to mark on her forehead—a rough outline of some kind of spider or something."

"No!"

"It's true," he said, taking a deep breath. "Sounds as if she might have been killed by some sort of lunatic. That's funny in a grim way, since she was insane herself."

"She said her husband was plotting to kill her," Diana recalled.

"Put that down to her madness," Brian said. "Whoever did this was some transient who must have met her wandering out on the grounds at night. The doctor has given us strict orders against this, but nobody pays attention."

Diana was reeling from a series of shattering thoughts. The murdered girl had been stabbed to death, according to Brian's report, and the memory of that blood-stained weapon on her dresser flashed before her mind. Was it possible she'd committed another violent crime during her blackout? She couldn't believe it. It seemed much more likely that someone else had craftily done the murder and then left the weapon in her room to incriminate her. She had to believe that! She had to hold on to that to keep her sanity!

She saw that Dr. Meyer and Dr. Decker were coming in the front door together. Then the two doctors came over to stand sternly before her and Brian.

Dr. Meyer said, "You are finally downstairs, Miss Collins."

"Yes," she said in a small voice, conscious that both doctors were studying her.

"You have heard what has happened?" he demanded.

"Yes."

"Because of the tragedy, our entire routine here will be disrupted," the senior doctor said sternly. "We had given strict orders to Mrs. Fenway never to leave Turn-bridge House at night, but she didn't listen."

"Have you any idea who did it?" Diana questioned him in a taut voice.

He shook his head. "No. But it must have been some demented person with a strong belief in astrology. Wouldn't you agree, Dr. Decker?"

He nodded. "Yes. I'm sure the rough drawing left on the victim's forehead was a scorpion. It would have to relate to the sign Scorpio."

Brian looked puzzled. "I don't remember that Mrs. Fenway had a special belief in the value of astrology."

"Nor do I," Dr. Meyer said. "We discussed many things, but astrology was not among them." He glanced over at her. "If I remember correctly you are the astrology fan, Miss Collins."

"Yes," she managed.

His shrewd eyes were studying her, and she wondered if there suddenly wasn't a glint of suspicion in them. He said, "And as I recall it, you are also a Scorpio like myself?"

"That is true," she said in a low voice.

Dr. Max Decker spoke up in his accented fashion, "This astrology belief is so widespread these days. Many intelligent people as well as the unstable have found

64

it appealing. That bizarre drawing isn't going to be much help in locating the murderer."

"I'm afraid not," Dr. Meyer agreed.

Brian asked. "Has the weapon been located?"

"No," Dr. Meyer said. "But I am sure the police will find it. You may as well be prepared for questioning. I'm sure they'll want to talk to all of you." And with that prediction he and the elderly Dr. Decker went on to the rear of the building and the offices.

When they were alone again, Brian Dale gave Diana a bleak look. "I can imagine the police giving us a real grilling. They never have much patience with loonies. That is what we all are in the minds of outsiders."

"At least they can't blame Paul Miles," she said. "He was locked up downstairs."

"You're wrong," Brian said. "He improved enough under drugs to be returned to his own room early last night. Hope went by to talk to him. He'll be in the forefront of the suspects."

"I didn't know," she said.

"And there's Barnabas Collins," Brian went on. "He was over at Collinwood until late last night. He'll have some explaining to do, since he must have been returning about the time that poor woman was killed."

She frowned. "Barnabas couldn't be guilty!"

"Why not?" Brian asked. "Any of us could be responsible. I had no idea Dr. Meyer took an interest in astrology."

"He at least knows the sign under which he was born."

"I've heard Dr. Ayler discuss it," Brian said. "He seemed to be a kind of expert on the subject."

"Really?"

"Yes. But then he dabbled in a lot of that occult stuff when he was in Los Angeles, according to his stories."

"I've never had much talk with him," Diana confessed unhappily.

At that moment the front door opened, and Carol came in looking poised and attractive in a white tennis outfit. She gave Diana a warning glance while Brian's back was still turned her way, then when Brian swung around to greet her, she smiled at him.

"It's a wonderful warm morning after the fog," she said. And to Diana, "You should be outside enjoying it."

"Your sister, like me, has been too shocked by the news of Hope Fenway's murder to think about the fine morning," Brian told her reprovingly.

Carol didn't appear at all upset by his words or tone. "Days like this are so rare in October we shouldn't ignore them. Dr. Ayler had promised me a game of tennis before the tragedy broke, and he managed to get enough time off to keep his word."

"Interesting," Brian said dryly, suggesting that this merely proved his dim opinion of the doctor.

Carol looked directly at Diana. "I insist you come outside for at least a short walk in the sun. You need it. Brooding here about what happened isn't going to change anything."

Diana knew why Carol had to see her alone so urgently. She gave Brian a plaintive look. "I guess she's right," she said. "I'll see you later. Let me know if you hear anything new."

"I will," he promised with another sigh. "Though from this point on, you'll probably hear things as quickly as I will."

Diana joined her sister and they went out the front door. Carol waited until they were a short distance from the house, then glancing back over her shoulder to make sure no one had followed them, she told Diana, "I got rid of the knife."

"Where?"

"An old well on the grounds," she said. "It's partly covered and boarded up, but I found an open crevice and got rid of it."

"The police will search and find it!"

"Not there!" Carol sounded positive. "I don't think they'll ever look for it there."

"Whoever used it murdered Hope," Diana said.

They halted and Carol said, "Yes, I realize that."

Diana stared at her in consternation. "You still believe that I was the one responsible?"

"What else can I think?"

She gazed into her sister's unrelenting face and found herself near tears. "I couldn't have done it!"

"The knife was on your dresser."

"I don't know how it got there!"

"You had one of your blackouts."

"That doesn't have to mean I'm a murderess!"

Carol looked noncommittal. "I can't forget what you did to Graham."

"That was different!"

"I don't see how," Carol told her. "At any rate, this is not the place or the time to go over it all. I merely wanted to tell you I'd gotten the knife disposed of. I'm doing my best to help you."

"You should at least have some belief in me," she begged.

Carol's blue eyes were cold. "It's past that. I know you are mentally unstable," she said. "I have to be realistic. All I can do is try and protect you."

Near tears, she said, "If I believed as you do . . . if I thought I were a murderess, I'd go to Dr. Meyer and confess!"

"I'd call that very silly," Carol said, "unless you want to be placed in some madhouse for the rest of your life."

"Please don't say such things!"

"We have to face facts. I'm trying to help you. You'd be wise to leave it at that!"

"But I'm in torment!" Diana protested. "I feel sure I'm innocent, but everything points to my guilt!"

"I'm glad you're aware of that," Carol said in her cool way. "And if the knife is found, I'll deny ever having seen it. You'll be on your own."

"Of course I don't want to implicate you," she agreed unhappily.

"You won't. I'll see to that," Carol assured her. "Now I think we should part. You go for a short walk, and I'll return to the house. We don't want to be seen talking together too much. It could rouse suspicions."

"But I need someone to talk to!"

"Not now!" Carol said curtly.

Diana stood there numbed with fear and torment as her sister walked briskly back toward the old mansion. She studied the chic figure in the white tennis outfit and thought what a difference there was between them. Carol had always been the strong one. Selfish and cold, perhaps, but strong!

She stood in the warm sunlight and tried to collect her thoughts. She still had to cling to the hope that she hadn't been involved in Hope Fenway's murder, but the weapon had been in her room and the mark of Scorpio had even been drawn in lipstick on the victim's forehead.

Her declaration that she would offer a confession if she believed she was guilty had been sincere. But she didn't think this was so. She was almost certain that if she could somehow recall the missing two hours of her blackout she would discover she was blameless. Someone else had slain the redhead, and why not Dr. Nils Ayler? He had the cruel, cold temperament of a killer, and Brian had mentioned that he was versed in astrology.

If only she could find Barnabas and talk to him. She had a deep conviction that he alone would be able to fill her in on some of the mystery of the previous night. But where to find him? To the left she saw a dark sedan and several members of the State Police, so she walked in the opposite direction. It must have been over there that the body of the unfortunate Hope had been found. Diana went close to the cliffs, and when she reached the edge, she stared down at the beach. There stood the dignified figure of Barnabas. Even without his caped coat she would have recognized him. He was staring out at the ocean with his back to her. She glanced back to where the police were and decided she dared not call out to him, there was too great a risk of being heard by the group that had converged on the spot where the body of Hope Fenway had been discovered. There was only one solution for her dilemma. She had to find the path to the beach.

She was ready to move along the edge of the cliffs in search of the path when she heard a footstep behind her. She turned to see Dr. Nils Ayler studying her with suspicious eyes.

The shaven-headed young man said, "If you have any idea of going down there and joining Barnabas Collins, I'd advise against it."

CHAPTER SIX

Diana was startled by the unexpected appearance of the young doctor and also by his blunt warning not to join Barnabas on the beach. She gave him a defiant glance, as her situation was much too desperate to give in easily now.

"Why shouldn't I speak to Barnabas if I wish?" she asked.

Ayler's cruel face showed annoyance. "You must be aware that a murder has been committed here and all the patients, including yourself, are under suspicion."

"I should think that would include everyone in the house," she said with meaning.

He frowned. "I'm warning you that it may look strange to the police if they see you and Barnabas Collins down there exchanging confidences. They might decide you two had something to do with Hope Fenway's murder."

"I doubt that," she said. "I often talk to Barnabas. And what reason is there for not doing it now?"

He shrugged. "You can do as you like, but don't come whining to me or Dr. Meyer if the police tackle you."

"I promise you I won't do that," she said.

"We'll see," he sneered.

She left him and hurried along the cliffs until she came to a path. When she was about halfway down it, she saw Barnabas turn and look her way. She waved and he waved back. At the same time she glanced toward the cliffs. Nils Ayler was still there, watching her.

The last couple of feet of the path were almost a straight drop. She raced down them so as not to stumble. Then she stood before Barnabas breathlessly.

"I came down to see you strictly against Dr. Ayler's orders," she laughed.

Barnabas glanced toward the cliffs with mild annoyance. "What right has he to tell you what to do?"

"He's a member of the staff, and I'm a patient," she said.

"That only applies under certain circumstances," Barnabas told her, an angry light in his brown eyes. "You should have the freedom of the grounds without interference from him or anyone else."

"A murder has been committed, and he says that changes things."

Barnabas looked serious. "It does. But I don't think it gives him the right to bully you."

"I've been wanting to talk with you," Diana went on.

"And I've been worried about you," he said.

Excitement rose in her. "What about?"

"Last night."

"Then you did find me?"

"Yes."

Her whole manner was eager. "So it was you who saved me from the werewolf and took me safely up to my room?"

He looked surprised. "I didn't see any monster, but I found you stretched out on the ground in a kind of coma. I assumed you'd been hit by one of your spells."

"I did have one," she admitted, "but it was caused by fright. A monster, like a wolf with burning amber eyes, stalked me."

"I didn't see any such creature," Barnabas said. "But when I found you I decided the best thing to do was get you to your room and your bed."

"And you carried me upstairs?"

"Yes," he said tensely. "I placed you on the bed, and then I left you to emerge from your spell. How long did it last?"

"Nearly two hours," she said. "Then I came to."

"Nasty."

"It was," she agreed with a solemn look on her pretty face. "I mean, especially when you think what I awoke to."

He furrowed his brow. "You mean Hope's murder? You couldn't have learned about that until this morning."

"No," she said. "Something else."

"What?"

She glanced up toward the cliffs and saw that Dr. Nils Ayler had gone and there was no one else watching them. Quickly, she went on, "I want to tell you everything before we're questioned, and I don't think we have much time."

"Go on," Barnabas told her.

"When I came to, last night, Carol joined me. She talked for a few minutes. We had a kind of argument. Then, when she was on her way out of the room, she discovered a knife on my dresser."

"A knife!" Barnabas echoed in surprise.

"Yes." She paused. "A blood-stained knife!"

The gaunt handsome face registered shock. "How did it get there?"

"I don't know. Carol at once jumped to the conclusion I put it there. She can't forget that I stabbed Graham Weeds when I had my first blackout and she doesn't seem to want to consider the special conditions surrounding the attack. He had goaded me into it. Just before I had the lapse of memory, he cruelly broke off our engagement and told me he was in love with Carol."

"That's past history and doesn't worry me," Barnabas told her. "But this knife with the bloodstains suggests trouble. Have you no memory of it?"

"None. I remember that wolf-like animal attacking me, and that's all."

"But Carol thinks you killed Hope during your memory lapse?"

"That's about it," she said unhappily.

"You had no knife when I found you," Barnabas told her. "And it was I who carried you up to your bed. If there had been a knife on the dresser, I would surely have noticed it."

These were exactly the words Diana wanted to hear. She told him, "I've felt all along I didn't do it. But Carol seems convinced I'm guilty, and she almost made me believe it."

"Don't allow her to do that."

"It's difficult when you're not sure," she said despairingly, "and those two hours are a blank to me."

"You probably just remained on the bed where I left you," Barnabas said. "The shock of seeing whatever it was you saw must have made you pass out."

"The werewolf!"

"Probably a stray mongrel," Barnabas said. "I don't think I'd mention it if the police should question you. Say you were in your room all evening. They are not liable to take very kindly to any story about werewolves."

"Whatever you think best," she said.

"What happened to the knife?"

"Carol took it."

"And . . ."

"She hid it. Dropped it down an abandoned well not far from Turnbridge."

Barnabas looked bleak. "The chances are the police will probably locate it. They'll search everywhere, and an abandoned well is a likely spot. She should have done something else with it. It's going to be awkward if your fingerprints or hers show on it."

"She carried it with a hankie," Diana said. "And I can't believe my prints are on it."

"Let's hope not," Barnabas said grimly. "This could be a very bad business."

"The murderer must have deliberately placed that knife in my room to make it seem I was the guilty one."

"It looks that way," he agreed. "And that suggests whoever killed Hope was watching when I carried you up the stairs to your room."

"They knew I'd had a blackout."

"And so you were a natural to blame for the murder," Barnabas concluded in a worried voice. "I can see that I was wrong."

"Why?"

"I should have alerted one of the doctors or your sister about your condition," he said worriedly. "Then you would have had care and there wouldn't be this uncertainty about what you did during the period when your mind was blank."

"I know I didn't kill Hope."

"So do I," Barnabas said. "But it's the police who must be convinced. Not that I expect it will come to that. They'll question you along with the rest of us, but I don't

72

imagine they'll be especially suspicious of you—not unless Carol should tell them about the knife."

"She won't."

"She can't. Not after making herself an accessory by trying to dispose of it. But still she might give it away without meaning to. The police can be tricky in their questioning."

She stared at him with frightened eyes. "Who do you think killed poor Hope, and why?"

"I wish I knew. I can only hazard a guess. It could be Paul Miles. They had him in solitary most of the day and then let him out last night. I think that was a mistake."

"So do I," she agreed. "He was very violent when I was locked in that cell with him."

"As a second suspect, why not consider the one who locked you in that lunatic's cell? We'd about decided it was Ayler."

"Why would Ayler want to harm Hope Fenway?"

"Hope always kept telling everyone there was a plot to kill her. Maybe her husband had made an arrangement with Ayler," Barnabas theorized.

"That sounds as mad as the stories she used to tell," Diana said.

"Murder is a mad business," Barnabas told her. "There's something about Ayler I don't like. I don't think he's all he pretends to be."

"I know he's cruel and crafty," she said bitterly.

"He's proved that."

"Very likely he was the one who threw you in that cell for the sheer pleasure of torturing you," Barnabas said. "I don't doubt he is capable of worse things."

She gave a deep sigh. "What will happen next?"

"The police questioning," Barnabas told her. "Do you think you can stand up to it?"

"Only because I believe I'm innocent," she said, "and because what you've told me backs up my belief. If I thought I'd stabbed Hope with that knife, I wouldn't want to go free. I'd want to be locked up where I could do no more harm."

"And that's what your sister is trying to make you believe. That you are guilty."

Diana considered this unhappily. "Carol isn't gifted with much imagination. It's easy for her to picture me as the killer because of what happened before."

"Which makes her a danger during the investigation," Barnabas said in a troubled voice. "I suppose we shouldn't stay down here together too long."

"I suppose not."

He patted her on the arm. "You must be brave. Remember that someone has tried to frame you for this tragic business. Fight back, and don't let them have their little game work out."

"I'll try," she said.

They left the beach and the feeling of security it offered. Diana became increasingly nervous as they walked up the path to the cliffs. She felt that very shortly they'd be facing a third degree by the police, and she didn't relish the prospect. Barnabas appeared quiet and subdued, so she knew he, too, was worried.

When they arrived at Turnbridge House, they were involved in the police investigation at once. The middle-aged state trooper who was in charge of the questioning had taken over Dr. Meyer's office. One at a time the patients were brought in for him to interview. When they left him, they were at once sent to their own rooms and so had no opportunity to discuss what had gone on with any of the others.

Diana waited her turn soberly with the others. The doctors, including Dr. Meyer, stood around with gloomy expressions on their faces. She could tell they were worried about the future of the clinic. The press was bound to get some of the details, and a story of this sort could spoil the work it had taken Dr. Meyer years to build.

When it came her turn, she was quietly polite to the white-haired police officer. She answered only the questions he asked and volunteered no other information. She could tell he was frustrated and reaching out to find some clues, but she made no attempt to help. She told him she'd been in her room all evening and hadn't seen Hope at any time.

The officer was studying her attentively as he asked her a blunt question, "Miss Collins, would you consider yourself a dangerous psychotic?"

74

Startled, she replied, "No, I wouldn't say so."

"Why are you here?"

"I'm very nervous. And my nervousness brings on memory blackouts. Dr. Meyer hopes to help me."

"Then you wouldn't consider yourself as demented as Paul Miles or Dawn Walsh?"

"No."

"I see," he said. "And you have nothing else you wish to tell me?" He gave her the impression he knew that she could help him if she wished. She surmised it was a bluff on his part and decided to be wary.

"Nothing," she said quietly.

"I hope for your own sake you're not concealing anything," the police officer said.

"I liked Hope Fenway," she assured him. "I'd like to help capture her murderer."

"Especially as he could be a threat to you as well," the man warned her.

"I realize that."

He looked down at some papers on his desk. "You have a sister here," he said, reading from the file without glancing up.

"Yes."

"But she is not a patient."

"No."

He gave her a probing glance. "I must have a chat with your sister, Miss Collins. I consider it unusual that she should be here."

"She didn't want me to be alone," Diana said. She tried to sound calm, but her nerves were jangling.

"I see," he said quietly. Then his shrewd eyes met hers once more. "Do you believe in ghosts, Miss Collins?"

"That's a hard question to answer directly," she said.

"Try."

"I can't," she told him. "I believe in the supernatural, but my interpretation of ghosts might be different from yours."

"This is an area where there are legends of vampires and werewolves. There are even some of the fisher folk along this lonely coast who will swear they've been visited by such creatures in these modern days."

"I doubt if time means anything to ghosts," she told him.

He smiled. "That could be true. You undoubtedly know the legend of Turnbridge House—the story of the cloaked beauty who appears to warn residents of the house of their approaching deaths?"

"Yes."

"Do you think it possible you might have seen her?" he asked casually.

"No," she said, not knowing what he might be leading to.

He looked down at his desk again with a frown. "Hope Fenway claimed that she saw this ghost and that several times the legendary lady had warned her she was soon to die."

Diana said, "Hope didn't mention the ghost to me."

He looked at her very directly. "Did she ever say anything to you about someone going to kill her?"

She knew at once there was no point in evading the truth. Some of the others had no doubt quoted Hope, and he was now trying to test her and see if she'd admit what she'd heard.

She said, "Several times she said there was a plot to kill her and that her husband was behind it. But I didn't pay any attention to her. I put it down as due to her mental state."

The officer listened quietly, then said, "Have you any suggestions as to who might be the guilty party?"

"No."

"Thank you, Miss Collins," he said. "That will be all for now, though it is possible I may wish to question you later."

She left the office feeling a new uneasiness. She had an idea he had heard something to make him suspect her but she didn't know what it was or who might have told him. On Dr. Meyer's stern instructions she went directly to her own room without speaking to anyone. There she sat in silence.

It seemed an age passed, and then she heard her door handle turn. She looked up to see Carol coming into the room. Her sister made a sign for her to say nothing. Next she closed the door and came quickly across the room.

In a whisper, Carol asked, "How did you make out?"

"I don't know. All right, I hope."

Carol's blue eyes were anxious. "Did they question you a lot?"

"Yes."

"Were you careful?"

She nodded. "I tried not to say much of anything."

Carol sighed in relief. "That was smart. He gave me a regular third degree. Couldn't seem to understand why I'd chosen to come here with you."

"He asked me about that," she admitted.

Her sister frowned. "Do you think he suspects you?"

"No. No more than anyone else here."

"Likely not," Carol agreed. "He doesn't know about your blackout or the knife. Then there'd be a difference."

Diana gave Carol a plaintive look. "I'm more certain than ever I didn't kill Hope. I think the knife was deliberately planted in my room by the murderer."

Carol's eyes and mouth opened wide. "Why are you so certain?"

"I talked with Barnabas."

"Barnabas!" Carol said scornfully.

"He had good news," she went on. "It was he who found me unconscious in the garden and brought me up to my room and placed me on the bed. He said there was no sign of a knife anywhere."

"How could he be sure?"

"That's what he said."

Carol looked angry. "I've heard enough stories about your wonderful Barnabas to put little stock in what he says. It could be he murdered Hope. It's not too long ago that he was asked to leave Collinsport because he was supposed to have attacked some village girls."

"I don't believe it!"

"I've had it on good authority. One of the doctors told me."

"Dr. Ayler, I suppose," she said indignantly.

"What if it was him?"

"He enjoys being nasty. And he's always making up stories about Barnabas!"

Carol smiled coldly. "When you see Barnabas again, ask him what happened the last time he visited Collinsport. Maybe he'll tell you." And with that cryptic remark she turned and left the room.

Diana remained by herself in an upset state. It was nearly one o'clock when Max Decker came to call on her. He was in his usual apologetic mood. "Forgive me for intruding, Miss Collins," he said.

"I'm glad to see anyone," she told him. "Are we going to have to stay in our rooms alone much longer?"

"No," he said. "The police have left, for the time being. Dr. Meyer wants all the patients to gather in the dining room for a buffet lunch and a general discussion."

She was instantly on her feet. "About the murder?"

"Yes. A most distressing business. Dr. Meyer fears the bad publicity will force him to close the clinic."

"I doubt if it will be that bad."

"These things are always bad," the doctor said, his guttural accent more pronounced in his distress. "It is difficult to predict what will happen. Can you join us in the dining room in fifteen minutes?"

"Yes," she promised.

Everyone was gathered in the dining room, including Barnabas and the three doctors. There was a tense air in the room, but no general discussion was attempted until the buffet was well underway. Diana had helped herself to some of the fine food and a cup of coffee. Now she stood across the room from Barnabas with the still-dazed Paul Miles at her side as she waited to hear from Dr. Meyer.

At last he cleared his throat and said, "I know you've all been wondering about my reason for bringing you here this way."

Brian Dale gave him a bitter smile. "We're not all that insane, Doctor. We know it's about the murder."

The austere Meyer looked as if he resented this interruption, but then seemed to change his mind. He glanced at the playwright indulgently. "You have come out with it very directly, Dale. And I suppose that's the best way."

Barnabas Collins now spoke up, a hint of annoyance on his handsome face. "Isn't the investigation of the murder best left to the police, Dr. Meyer?"

Dr. Meyer frowned. "Of course it is. I have no thought of taking on that task. This meeting is for quite another purpose."

Now the world-weary Dawn Walsh addressed him. "Then why not explain your reason for herding us here?"

Dr. Nils Ayler gave her a glance of rebuke. "I'm sure the doctor will do that if you give him a chance."

Dr. Meyer cleared his throat. "Exactly," he said, looking around at all of them. "I feel I should warn you that the police seem to believe one of you is responsible for the killing."

Brian Dale laughed bitterly. "I'd say we all knew that from the start."

"Naturally, I don't share this view," Dr. Meyer said. "I'm extremely sorry that you're suffering this additional ordeal. You have come here for quiet and treatment, and this is hardly likely to be helpful."

Barnabas seemed genuinely frustrated. "But you must have your own thought as to who killed Hope?"

Dr. Meyer looked apprehensive. "I never speak unless I'm certain. And I'm not certain in this case."

There was a short silence among them. Diana glanced over at Carol, who was standing very erect and looking pale. She then shifted her gaze to Paul Miles who she guessed must still be under heavy sedation. He stood like a zombie, yet his lips were moving nervously as if he were speaking to himself.

Dr. Meyer addressed them again, "I have a further worry. I believe the murder was done by an outsider who may strike again, and that means any of you could be the next victim."

Barnabas asked, "What about the lipstick drawing found on Hope's forehead?"

The doctor sighed. "That is one of my reasons for believing the murderer was someone outside Turnbridge Hall. I have an idea the crime was committed by some fanatic who is a strong believer in astrology. I don't think we have any such person here."

Dr. Ayler gave Diana a bitter mocking glance but said nothing. She felt her head start aching and began to worry about whether this was a warning of another of her spells. She hoped not. It would be the worst thing that could happen at this time. The mention of the lipstick drawing on the murdered girl's forehead had started her thinking. Did she have her lipstick with her when she went out the previous night? She sometimes carried an extra one in the pocket of her suit. She couldn't remember.

Dawn Walsh smiled faintly. "I don't think I need worry. The murderer is interested in beautiful women, and I am so ugly."

"I wouldn't take comfort in that," said Dr. Ayler. "You might be very wrong."

Diana remembered that Dawn had been suggested to her as a possible murder suspect. It wasn't all that unlikely. The former model was very mixed up and could have taken a dislike to Hope.

Max Decker was standing there, dejected and silent. Diana had an idea he was troubled about the future of the clinic. It might be difficult for him to find another position with equal pay and opportunities, especially if any of his prospective employers checked up on his Nazi career.

Dr. Meyer now was giving his attention to Carol. He told her, "I naturally think of you in this unhappy situation. While the others here are either staff or patients, you are a free agent. You can leave at once if you like. It seems to me you should."

Carol was very pale. "I wouldn't think of deserting my sister at this time."

Dr. Meyer frowned. "I don't see that your presence can make much difference one way or another."

Carol said, "If I leave, I will take Diana with me."

She spoke up, "There is no need of that. If Dr. Meyer thinks you'd be safer away from here, I say you should go."

"I've made up my mind," Carol said firmly.

Diana was distressed by her sister's decision but still couldn't help being grateful to her. There was no denying that in her own cold, harsh way she was doing the best she could.

Barnabas said, "Perhaps we are making too much of all this. It seems to me it would be better to let the police worry about it and carry on here as normally as possible."

Dr. Meyer smiled thinly. "You speak as if you were the staff director, Mr. Collins."

Barnabas shrugged. "I'm merely expressing an opinion."

"Perhaps as sound a one as may turn up," the doctor remarked.

At that moment one of the nurses showed herself in the doorway and rather nervously said, "The Inspector would like to speak with you a moment, Dr. Meyer."

"You will excuse me," he said to them all and quickly went out.

There was an air of tension in the room. Barnabas gave Diana a reassuring glance, and she tried to take courage from it. But her head was aching worse than ever. The murmurs of the voices around her were a torment, and she turned to look at Paul Miles, who seemed to be isolated from them all in his drugged, maniacal state. Surely he would be better off in the quiet of his own room than at this gathering. And so would she, though the solitude of the morning had palled on her.

Now Dr. Meyer came back into the room again, and there was a grim expression on his thin face. She could tell he had some important information to convey.

Standing in the middle of the big room he told them, "They have found the knife that was the murder weapon."

CHAPTER SEVEN

This announcement came as a bombshell in the well-filled room. Diana gave her sister a look of distress, but Carol showed no expression at all. It seemed she must have nerves of iron. The others were murmuring their surprise and interest.

Dr. Meyer went on, "The police have studied the weapon for fingerprints but found none. Whoever the killer was apparently was careful to wear gloves of some sort. But the blood type of the stains on the weapon matched that of Mrs. Fenway."

Diana felt a deep relief at hearing there had been no fingerprints. She'd worried that Carol might have inadvertently left some on the knife, despite her precautions, and there was also the devastating possibility that her own fingerprints might have been on it, if she had committed the crime in her blacked-out state. The fact that they weren't was more encouraging evidence of her innocence —at least, it seemed so to her.

Dr. Meyer said, "The police will continue their investigations. The knife came from the kitchen here and I fear will reinforce their theory that one of us is responsible. While this state of tension continues, there will be no regular treatment periods. However, medical assistance will be available at all times. If any of you has a particular problem, do not hesitate to call on me."

The austere head of the clinic walked out with Dr. Nils Ayler accompanying him. This left the elderly Dr. Decker to cope with the group. He gave them a worried look from behind his thick-lensed glasses. "It would be best for you to remain in your rooms as much as possible, though some exercise around the house and grounds is not denied you. Be prepared at any time for more questioning."

The session broke up, and Barnabas at once came across the room to Diana and said, "The situation doesn't get any less complicated, does it?"

"No," she said, her head reeling so now that she was barely able to keep up a conversation.

Barnabas glanced around and in a low voice said, "I see that Dr. Decker is getting Paul Miles out of here fast. He shouldn't have been brought down at all. He's in a bad state."

"I agree," she managed.

He eyed her with alarm. "You look ill!" he said.

She touched a hand to her forehead. "One of those headaches again."

"Shouldn't you talk to one of the doctors about it?"

"I will," she promised. "I'll likely have a chance to speak to Dr. Decker on the stairs."

"You heard what Dr. Meyer said," Barnabas reminded her. "Don't take any chances. There could be another murder among us."

"Surely not!" she protested.

"I think he's right," Barnabas confided. "I believe Hope Fenway was killed by error, that the killer meant to finish off someone else."

Fighting the raging headache, she stared at him in bewilderment. "Why do you say that?"

"I have good reasons," Barnabas assured her. "I'll discuss them with you later."

"I'm going upstairs," she said.

He was studying her worriedly. "Do you want me to go with you?"

"No. I'll manage."

She left the room and made her way to the stairway. Then, grasping the railing, she slowly began the long ascent to the third floor. She paused twice along the way. When she reached the third landing, she came face to face with Dr. Decker.

"Are you feeling badly, Miss Collins?" he asked.

Diana stood clutching the newell post, the doctor's face swaying before her glazed eyes. "My head again," she murmured.

"Distressing," he worried. "No doubt the tension. Let me accompany you to your room."

She was too ill to offer any argument, so the doctor assisted her to her bedroom and helped her to the bed. There he took her temperature and puttered around finding the proper vial of tablets and a glass of water for her to take them with. This accomplished, he sat down by her bedside.

"Is the medication helping any?" he wanted to know.

She was resting with closed eyes. "Too soon to know," she said.

"It should help," he promised. "You are in no fit shape to be caught up in a dreadful situation such as we have here."

"Perhaps with some rest . . ." she said.

"Rest is vital for you," he agreed. "Paul Miles is also suffering from all that has happened. I feel we might have brought him back to normal if the murder hadn't taken place. Now he seems to be slowly drifting away from us again. His condition remains on the edge of violence."

She opened her eyes to look up at the agitated face of the old doctor. "If that is so, shouldn't he be sent away from here? He could be a menace to the rest of us."

"I suggested he be sent away, but Dr. Ayler disagreed," he said, a hint of despair in his tone. "Dr. Ayler can be very difficult when he wishes, and Dr. Meyer takes his advice far too often."

Diana listened with growing fear. Because of the unpleasant shaven-headed doctor, they were all being kept in close proximity to a dangerous lunatic. If Dr. Decker's opinion was correct, Paul Miles could explode into aggressive insanity at any time.

She ventured, "Perhaps Paul Miles is the killer. He had the opportunity."

The old German doctor looked startled. "You really think that?"

"Yes. He is quite mad. He could have taken a dislike to Hope."

"He could have," he agreed. "I sometimes think this is the wrong place for a psychiatric clinic. There are too many demons in this old house, too many evil spirits!"

Her head was easing a little. She looked at him with amazement. "You surely don't believe in ghosts and demons."

"When you reach my age you know there are many strange, unexplainable things," Dr. Decker said grimly. "I do not deny the supernatural."

Diana looked at him very directly. "The night of Hope's murder, I'm sure I saw a werewolf. I was out walking in the fog, and some huge thing with burning amber eyes came at me out of the shadows!"

Dr. Decker looked puzzled and Diana had the impression he thought she was raving. "Has the medicine helped?" he asked.

"Yes. It's beginning to work. My head is aching less."

"If we are fortunate, you will not have an attack," the doctor assured her. "Whenever you feel a spell coming on, take the tablets. In that way you can avoid having a blackout."

"I'll remember," she promised.

"You still should keep as quiet as possible. It would be excellent if you had a short sleep."

"I feel drowsy."

"That is good."

"But I can't forget about the murder."

He frowned. "That is not good. You will gain nothing from such worry, and perhaps make yourself really ill again."

"It's hard not to think about it," she said with a tiny shudder. "You are right—this house has more than its share of evil spirits."

Dr. Decker leaned close to her. "I agree with Dr. Meyer that it is not right for your sister to remain here."

"So do I, but Carol won't leave without me."

"Perhaps you both should go."

"No," she said. "I have this feeling that Dr. Meyer is my only hope to be normal again."

"That may well be true," Dr. Decker said.

"So I can't leave."

He sighed. "Then there is nothing to do about it."

"Carol may appear to be a cold person," Diana explained, "but she has a hidden quality of kindness and a feeling of responsibility."

"There was a difference between her and you about a young man," the doctor remarked.

"Yes," she said, "that is all in my file. We both were in love with the young lawyer who is handling our father's estate. He has turned to Carol. That marked the beginning of my breakdown."

"Yet you hold no hatred for your sister?" He was watching her with interested eyes.

"I don't believe so," she said. "It was one of those things. I have no right to blame her."

"You're showing admirable understanding."

Diana smiled wryly. "I doubt that. There are many things on which we don't agree. But she does want me to get well again."

Dr. Decker nodded. "That is what is most important, so you must not worry." He paused, then said, "If I tell you something, can I depend on you to keep it a secret?"

"I think so."

He glanced toward the door to make sure it was closed and then leaned close to her again. "The trouble going on here may soon be settled."

She raised herself on an elbow. "You mean the murder?"

He nodded, a crafty expression on his lined face. "Yes."

"You know who the guilty person is?"

"I have almost enough proof," Dr. Decker said.

Her eyes went wide with shock. "Then why don't you inform the police and get the investigation ended that much faster?"

He shook his head. "No. I have learned to be wary of the police. Back in Germany I was taught that lesson. I do not have enough evidence yet. To speak too soon might ruin everything."

"How long dare you wait? Dr. Meyer said the killer might strike again!"

"I will be watching for that," he assured her. "Now that I know who it is."

"It could be dangerous for you, too!"

He smiled. "Do not worry about me, Miss Collins. Just be very cautious yourself."

"Cautious of whom?"

He raised a warning forefinger. "I did not promise to tell you that. Now I must leave."

She was still sitting up on her bed. "But you have me really excited!"

"There is nothing you can do. Rest and wait!" he said as he left.

Diana lay down on the pillow again and stared up at the ceiling of the ancient bedroom. This partial revelation was tormenting for her. She couldn't decide whether Dr. Decker really knew who the killer was or whether he was merely guessing. He was a strange old man, yet she preferred him to the cruel Dr. Ayler. She closed her eyes and under the influence of the sedative soon dropped off to sleep.

When she opened her eyes, it was almost dark and a shadowy figure was at her bedside. She was about to cry out when she recognized that it was her sister, Carol.

"I thought you were a ghost," she told Carol.

"I've been worried about you," her sister said. "This is the first chance I've had to talk with you. I was going to come by earlier, but I saw that Dr. Decker was here."

"Yes. He gave me some medicine. It helped."

"Then you didn't have a blackout spell?"

"No."

"You looked dreadfully ill downstairs," Carol went on. It was impossible to see the expression on her face, but she kept her voice low. "I was afraid you might be going to blurt out everything."

"I honestly didn't know what might happen when I heard they'd found the knife!"

"I told you it would be all right."

"I was worried about fingerprints."

"I took care of that," Carol assured her. "But you looked so guilty I was sure everyone must have guessed you were the killer."

"But I'm not!" she protested.

"We still can't be positive about that!"

"I am," Diana said defiantly. "I know I didn't do it."

"And I hope not," her sister replied. "But I still want to protect you every way possible. I did find that knife in here."

"Somebody must have done that deliberately."

"So you say," Carol commented.

"I think the murder will soon be solved."

"Why do you say that?"

"Someone told me."

"Who? Barnabas Collins?"

"No."

"I should hope not. You mustn't trust that madman. For years he behaved like a vampire. He became so obsessed with the legends of Collinwood that he decided he was one of the living dead."

"I don't believe that," Diana said, getting up from the bed. "I asked him about it and he said it wasn't so."

Carol's tone was cold. "Do you expect him to tell you the truth?"

"Yes."

"You still know very little about men," was her sister's comment. "I had a phone call from Graham Weeds. He heard about the murder here, and he's very concerned about us."

"There is no need for you to remain. Even Dr. Decker agrees with that."

"I intend to stand by you," Carol said firmly. "Graham is driving down tomorrow afternoon to visit us. He seemed in such a state I told him he could come."

Diana sighed. "I'm not up to seeing him. You can talk to him."

"But he'll want to see you, too," Carol insisted. "He may not still be in love with you, but he does like you, and he still has charge of all our legal affairs."

Carol remained for a few minutes more and then left her alone again. Diana put on the lights and prepared for dinner. It was a somber occasion with both Paul Miles and Barnabas missing. Diana enquired about Barnabas from Brian Dale.

The playwright said, "He spoke to me about going over to Collinwood again. He spends a lot of time there."

"Are there police still stationed on the grounds?" Diana asked.

"I guess so," he said. "I don't know for certain."

Dr. Decker was very subdued during the meal, rarely speaking to anyone, while Dawn Walsh hardly stopped talking. She went on weirdly about her accident and kept harping on her lost beauty. Diana listened to her in astonishment, since the girl was still lovely, despite her few facial scars.

After dinner she saw Carol and Dr. Nils Ayler go into the living room and seat themselves in a remote corner. It struck her that it might be infatuation for the bizarre-looking young doctor, rather than concern for her, that was keeping her sister at the clinic despite the sinister turn of events. Diana wondered what Graham Weeds would think if he knew the arrogant psychiatrist and Carol were nearly always together.

She was standing a distance from the two watching them when Brian Dale came up beside her. In an insinuating tone, he suggested, "Could there be a budding romance there?"

Diana turned to him quickly. "Was it so obvious I was watching them?"

"I'm afraid so," he said. "They are pretty thick."

"I don't like him at all," she said. "But then that isn't so unusual. Carol and I agree on very few things."

"So I notice," the young man said. "How does it feel to be here in a house filled with evil?"

She gave him a wry smile. "You should know that as well as any of us."

"It's been good for me. I'm actually afraid someone will try to kill me. The reason I'm here is I've tried to take my own life, and suddenly being alive seems important. At least I want to make the decision whether I live or die."

Diana nodded. "I know what you mean."

"You're one of the few people I'm able to talk to," he said. "I'm glad you came here—though it may not be so good for you."

"You've been helpful to me," she told him.

"I want to be," he said earnestly. "Maybe that has been my trouble. I've been too much absorbed with myself. It's important to have some involvement with others, to be of some use to the group."

"That sounds like straight thinking."

"It follows a long series of twisted ideas," he said ruefully. "Perhaps now I can go back to society and take my place again. I'm beginning to feel I'd like to try."

Diana smiled. "I'm glad for you."

"What about you and your blackouts?"

She took a deep breath. "I almost had one this afternoon, but Dr. Decker gave me some medicine and I came out of it."

"That sounds as if they know how to help you."

"I'm sure they do," she said.

"Poor Hope!" he said with a frown. "I believe Dr. Meyer might have cured her if she hadn't been killed. I could see that she was gradually getting better."

"She expected to be killed. She claimed her husband was in on the plot."

"That was part of her madness," the playwright said. "He sent her here to be helped."

Diana began to feel weary. "It's not late, but I think I'll go up to bed."

Brian smiled wryly. "I'll bet if Barnabas were here you wouldn't feel so drowsy."

She blushed. "I'm sure I would."

"You like him, don't you?"

"I admire him as a fine man," she agreed.

"I think it's more personal than that," he ventured, "and I wish you luck. Just don't forget he has his weakness, too, or he wouldn't be a patient here."

"I'd say whatever weakness he may have once had he's conquered."

"Perhaps," he commented, but there was a strong hint in his manner that he didn't believe this to be true.

Diana went upstairs. The hall light at the third floor landing had apparently burned out, so she had to walk down the hallway in darkness. An odd feeling of danger came to her. It was as if an icy chill had come into the air. As she touched the knob of her door and prepared to enter her bedroom, the sensation became stronger.

She at once thought of Paul Miles. Was the crisis at hand? Had he finally shaken off the effects of the numbing sedation to become violent once again? It was a terrifying thought to know the stocky man might be in there waiting to attack her. Or could it be something else? Something in which the supernatural was involved? Brian Dale and Dr. Decker had both spoken of evil spirits in the old house. She had seen the werewolf that night in the fog, and there was that other phantom which was said to haunt Turnbridge Hall, the lonely lady who had long ago taken her own life.

These frightening possibilities raced through her mind, but she had no choice but to open the door. The room was black, and she moved toward the light switch, but before she could reach it, a weird figure stepped in front of her.

Diana gave a scream of alarm and stepped back.

"Don't be afraid!" came a familiar voice, and she knew it was merely Dawn Walsh in her room again.

"What are you doing in here in the dark?" she asked, still fearful since it had been suggested that Dawn might be the killer.

"I cling to the dark," the former model said. "I couldn't

stand it any longer down there with you all staring at me!"

"Why should we stare at you?"

"Because of my face. It's such a horror, isn't it?" the girl insisted.

"You know that isn't true!"

"Don't lie!" she demanded with such hatred that Diana began to think she could be dealing with a murderess.

"I'm not lying," she said calmly. "And I'm very weary. I don't want to stand here talking nonsense. I'm going to turn on the lights."

"No!" Dawn stood in her way.

"Do you want me to call one of the doctors?" Diana asked.

"Don't do that!"

"Then you must behave reasonably," she told her.

"Death is going to visit here again," she said in a sepulchral tone.

"Why do you say that?"

"I know it will happen!"

"How do you know?" Diana asked sharply.

"The ghost told me."

Diana was beginning to find how utterly impossible it was to reason with a demented mind, and felt that perhaps it was best to go along with the other girl in her fantasy. "What ghost?"

"You know the one. The Lost Lady."

"Have you seen her?"

"Many times," Dawn Walsh said, in a manner so convincing that again Diana felt a cold terror.

"You're just making that up," she reproved her.

"No. She came to me last night. She was wearing the cloak, just like they tell about her, and she whispered to me. She said that someone else was about to die. That was why she was making the visit."

Diana wondered whether some facts might be dragged out of her story. "Did she tell you who was going to die?"

"Maybe . . ." Dawn was suddenly discovering the relish of hugging a secret.

"Tell me, or I'll know you're making this all up," she said sharply.

Dawn darted back in the shadows. "No!"

"Why not?"

"The ghost will come back and do something to me if I tell," she wailed.

"I promise she won't!"

"You can't stop her! You're trying to trick me!" With these frightened declarations, the girl dodged by her and escaped out of the room.

Diana switched on the lights and closed the door. At least she was rid of her. She was beginning to have serious doubts about Dawn Walsh. It was possible she was not the pathetic, frightened creature she pretended to be. She could very well be the one responsible for Hope Fenway's murder, and now she might be planning another, judging from her talk. It came to Diana with a shock that she could very well be the insane girl's next target.

But then she dismissed the thought. From all she knew, and what Dr. Decker had hinted, she was ready to pick Paul Miles as the most likely suspect. Surely the police must be well aware of this also, and were keeping an eye on him, though there were no signs of police around on this dark night. Perhaps they went along with Dr. Meyer's theory that an outsider was to blame, though it had been suggested the police felt the murderer must be one of them.

It was all too confusing. She prepared for bed in a thoroughly nervous state. Tomorrow Graham Weeds would be arriving, and that would be an ordeal of another sort. He would insist on seeing her, and she had come to dislike him a lot. But because he was still acting for the estate, she could not completely avoid him.

Another intriguing question was to what extent Carol had fallen in love with the arrogant Nils Ayler. If this was turning into a serious romance, Graham Weeds might find himself without a fiancée! She thought this might be just payment for him. She had no intention of going back to him if he and Carol broke up. She'd discovered just how shallow the lawyer was.

Of course she disliked Dr. Ayler equally, so there was no choice. It was strange that Carol should be attracted to such men. Thinking about these things, she got into bed and turned out the lights, but her mind was much too active to settle down to sleep at once. She lay there a long while before her eyelids began to droop and her mind drifted off into a dream state.

Her dream was about that foggy night when she'd been confronted by the weird, grayish-yellow animal. The werewolf was as large and terrifying in her dream as it had been in the cold, gray mist of that eventful night. It crouched, and its burning amber eyes were fixed on her just as they had been then. She drew back with a scream as it sprang toward her. Its great body knocked her to the ground. She screamed and lifted her hands to fight the monster off as its slavering mouth and yellowed fangs pressed close to her . . .

And then she heard the voice of Barnabas. She couldn't tell what he was saying, but he was calling out in a loud, angry fashion. Strangely, it halted the attack on her. The beast drew back with more low snarling and then turned and ran off into the thick fog. As it vanished, she raised herself on an elbow and sobbing, looked around to see Barnabas.

But Barnabas was nowhere in sight. Struggling to her feet, she started to walk to the house when another figure stepped out of the shadows to threaten her!

This time it was the shaven-headed Dr. Nils Ayler.

The cruel-faced young man sneered at her. "You're not getting away so easily!"

"Barnabas is here!" she told him. "He'll save me!"

"Barnabas is not here!" he said mockingly, and he stretched out a hand to grasp her. The sight of it made her scream out again—for the hand was a skeleton hand! The fingers, bony fingers!

Diana kept screaming, and then she awoke to the darkness of her bedroom. The panic she'd felt in the dream was still with her. She sat up in bed suddenly. The menace she'd known in her nightmare was still in this room. She somehow sensed it.

Then she saw the figure silently coming toward her—a figure in a flowing cape. Thoughts of the Lost Lady of Turnbridge flashed through her mind. Had the legendary ghost come to warn her of her impending death? Was she to be the next murder victim?

Before she could pursue these thoughts further, the shadowy phantom was upon her. As she screamed her

fear and fought back, strong hands gripped her throat.
Strong, icy hands that sent a chilling message to her tortured mind. These were surely skeleton hands! Bony,
skeleton fingers tightening grimly around her throat and
shutting her off from life!

CHAPTER EIGHT

The sound of heavy breathing, tortured breathing that
spoke of pain and suffering! Dots of light flashed in the
darkness . . . and then vanished. Diana stirred a little and
became aware of the burning of her throat and the dull
throb in her head. Staring into the shadows, she remained
in a state of dazed apathy. Until at last memory began
to return to her . . . the macabre skeleton fingers at her
throat!

Diana sat up with a gasp that was partly a sob of fear.
The attack on her by the phantom became clear in her
mind, and now she was filled with a desire to escape from
the confines of the dark bedroom and seek help. She'd
been the target of either a ghost or some insane creature.
Swinging out of bed, she made her way through the darkness to the door leading to the hallway.

There was a dim light outside normally, but as she'd
noticed earlier, it had burned out. Now only a ghostly ray
of light from the landing below seeped up the stairwell. She
moved slowly along the hallway toward the faint light. Her
mind was still confused, but she had some sort of plan to
find Barnabas and enlist his aid. She vaguely believed
his room was on the same floor, but in the other wing of
the old mansion.

She'd gone partly along the hall when she saw the bent
form of Max Decker on the stairway. He was almost to
the landing, and she felt a surge of hope, certain he would
help her. She was about to call out to him when suddenly

from the shadows of the landing a cloaked figure revealed itself. It happened so quickly, and the figure was so swathed in some dark flowing material, that Diana had no idea who it might be.

But apparently Dr. Decker saw the face of the ghostly one as he clutched the newell post. His lined face showed an expression of surprise and fear. At the same instant the apparition hurled itself on the old man and sent him sprawling backward down the stairs. Diana was frozen with horror. The phantom vanished in the shadows again, and a cloak of blackness descended on Diana's mind.

She was shivering with cold, and the roar of the waves sounded loud in her ears. Staring around her, she saw that she was standing in the gardens of Turnbridge House. It was the edge of dawn, by the appearance of the sky. Trembling with chill again, she saw that she was clothed only in her flimsy nightgown and her feet were bare. The dampness of the grass sent a further chill through her.

She had had another blackout! There was no question of that. And she'd wandered out into the night again. Her teeth chattered as she clutched her arms about her and considered her abject state. In the distance the gloomy old mansion loomed, a brooding shadow against the growing light of the sky. The sight of it made her recall those last terrifying minutes before she'd lost contact with reality.

A phantom had appeared out of the shadows and hurled Dr. Decker down the stairway! That was the last thing she recalled. How long she'd been in a blank state would have to remain a question, but it was probably for a long while, and she had wandered out here heedless of the dampness and chill. Now she must somehow get back inside and see what had happened and whether Dr. Decker was hurt badly.

At this point she couldn't be certain that it hadn't all been a mad nightmare. Her lovely face was white and drawn as she turned and started back to Turnbridge House. But she halted almost immediately as a threatening figure appeared in her path, blocking the way. The blurred outline of the insane, stocky Paul Miles made her cry out in terror.

"No!" the mad architect croaked hoarsely, taking a step nearer her.

"Go away!" she pleaded.

"Louise!" he said in an odd voice that clearly indicated he was lost in dementia once again.

"I'm not your Louise!" she said fearfully.

He paid no attention to her and continued to move toward her. The small eyes in his broad, beard-stubbled face glittered madly. Coming close, he reached out and took her by the arms. She stared at him in horror as she tried to think of some way to escape from him.

Then the sound of a quick footstep behind her gave her some hope. The crisis dissolved as the voice of Barnabas Collins rang out sternly, "Miles, what are you doing?"

The blank face of the madman took on a dazed expression, and he released her at once. Then, glancing at her for a brief moment, he turned and hurried away in the direction of the house. By that time Barnabas was at her side.

"What does all this mean?" he asked.

Diana looked up into his handsome face despairingly and through chattering teeth told him, "I had a blackout and wandered out here."

Barnabas was all concern. He quickly removed his caped coat and draped it over her shoulders. "That will at least keep you warm," he said.

Diana wavered slightly. "A phantom came to my room and attacked me. I went out into the hall and saw Doctor Decker on the stairs."

Barnabas was frowning. "Are you sure you didn't dream all this? That the nightmare wasn't part of your blackout?"

"No," she protested weakly.

"Go on."

"The phantom appeared in the hallway and hurled the doctor down the stairs. Then I went blank."

"It's a wild story," Barnabas told her. "So you don't know how you got out here, or what Paul Miles has to do with it?"

"No, I just saw Paul a few minutes ago." Her whole body was trembling.

Barnabas looked down at her bare feet. "You have no slippers on."

"I was looking for you," she said plaintively.

"I spent the night at Collinwood," he said. "I've been looking into some matters. It was easier to do it over there."

"I didn't know." Her head was spinning, and she feared she might faint.

Barnabas became aware of her condition and quickly swept her up in his arms. "I'll take you inside and we'll try to find out what has gone on."

She nodded without making any reply. Barnabas carried her without effort, and she felt a small feeling of security as she clung to the handsome Britisher. She was beginning to fear what they might discover when they entered the old mansion. Was it possible that all she'd experienced had been a fantastic nightmare? If so, it suggested her own mental state might be worsening.

Barnabas took her in through the front door and deposited her gently on a chaise longue in the living room. It was dawn, and the elegantly furnished room was filled with a gray light. He at once left her and went to the sideboard at the opposite end of the room. Shortly after, he returned with a glass of amber liquid in his hand.

Offering it to her, he said, "Drink that. It will warm you. Meanwhile, I'll make an investigation of the house."

"Please," she begged him and took the glass.

She drank some of the burning liquid while Barnabas went to see what he could find out. The house was still very quiet; apparently none of the servants or nursing staff were up yet. The drink revived her a good deal and stopped her trembling, so that when Barnabas returned a few minutes later, she was able to take in fully what he had to tell her.

His gaunt, handsome face revealed shock as he stood before her. "You were right," he said.

She sat up. "What about Dr. Decker?"

"I found his body sprawled on the second landing," Barnabas said gravely, "at the foot of the stairway. He must have broken his neck."

"It was no accident," she protested. "I saw what happened. The phantom pushed him."

"So it seems," Barnabas said, staring at her oddly.

She sensed there was more. "Go on," she said.

"Someone drew the Scorpio design on his forehead with a lipstick," he said. "Just the same as they did with Hope Fenway. So that suggests the two deaths are associated."

Diana sprang to her feet. "But that's mad!"

"I'd say it was the work of an insane person," Barnabas agreed. "If it weren't for what you've told me, and that rough Scorpio outline on his forehead, I'd be inclined to say his death was accidental. That he'd fallen."

"No!"

"There's no doubt you're right," Barnabas said with a sigh. "He was murdered."

"I saw it happen."

He studied her anxiously. "One thing worries me. If you tell the others this wild story about a phantom attacking you and then Dr. Decker, they're apt to get the idea it is a mad concoction of yours and maybe decide you're the murderess, that it was you, during one of your spells, who hurled the old man down the stairs."

"I wouldn't do such a thing!" she protested.

"I know that," he said worriedly. "I believe in you, but others may not be so considerate. It's something to think about."

Diana was filled with new panic. "But I can't keep silent, I have to tell what I saw."

"It's probably the best way," he said reluctantly. "And yet there will be a hazard to it."

Her eyes widened. "Don't you think I should tell the truth?"

Barnabas looked troubled. "Yes."

"There's no other way!"

"I suppose not," he agreed heavily. "I think you should go to your room and try to collect yourself while I inform the others what has happened."

"You think it's going to be bad?" she asked, filled with apprehensions.

"I'm afraid so. It will bring the police back. This time, they'll not doubt that some of us are responsible."

"What about Paul Miles?"

"It could have been him," Barnabas agreed. "You

98

haven't told me whether this phantom was a man or woman."

"I don't know," she said miserably. "All I have is a confused picture of a shadowy figure in a flowing cloak with its head covered by a hood!"

"Which is no help at all."

"It's all I can tell you."

Barnabas said, "You'll have to be prepared for a lot of questioning. It will be an ordeal. As I see it now, you're going to be the chief murder suspect."

She gazed at him with startled eyes. "But that's so unfair! I was very fond of Dr. Decker. I considered him the best-natured member of the staff. I was about to ask him for aid last night when the phantom attacked him."

"I understand that," Barnabas said. "I only hope you can make the others see it."

"You sound so pessimistic!"

"I have learned to be cautious over the years," Barnabas told her. "People are not intelligent—or even kind—when it comes to things like this. They are bound to reject any supernatural explanation offered by you for a logical answer. Since you admit to having been on the scene and suffering a spell right afterwards, you'll be the scapegoat. Insanity is automatically associated with guilt in our society, wrong as that may be."

"What can I do?" she asked, feeling trapped.

"Nothing but give your account of what you saw just as you've given it to me," he said. "And be careful you have the details exactly the same each time you tell it."

"My mind is in chaos," she said wearily, her exhaustion suddenly catching up with her.

"Let me help you upstairs," Barnabas said. "We'd better use the back stairway. No use subjecting you to the sight of the body. Besides it's better to keep away from there until the police come."

She let him guide her down the hall to the rear of the old house and the steep back stairs. Nothing was said by either of them as they mounted the stairs. Then Barnabas escorted her down the hallway to the door of her room.

Hesitating there, he said, "I'd better stop by your sister's room and ask her to come to you."

She sighed. "I don't know. Sometimes she upsets me."

"I don't think you should be alone," Barnabas said.

She looked up into his concerned face. "I'll do whatever you say," she told him. She meant it. She had no one else she could completely depend on now.

Barnabas studied her with gentle eyes. "I hope this won't be too difficult for you," he said. He drew her close and kissed her on the forehead. Then he told her, "Go inside, and I'll send Carol to you."

Diana had washed and changed into a dress by the time Carol joined her. Her sister was still in her dressing gown. She looked shocked. Facing Diana, she asked, "What is all this I hear from Barnabas?"

"It's true," she said. "A phantom attacked me and then killed Dr. Decker. I had a blackout immediately after, and Barnabas found me wandering in the garden."

"The Scorpio sign!" Carol said fearfully.

"What about it?"

"Barnabas said he found it again on Dr. Decker's forehead! Marked there in lipstick, just as it was with Hope Fenway!"

She spread her hands. "I can't help that!"

"You know what it means?"

"No."

Carol's face was deathly white. "You are a Scorpio!"

"What of it?"

"Your sign was left on both victims," her sister said accusingly. "Why did you do it?"

Diana stared at her incredulously. "I didn't do it!"

Carol came up and grasped her by the arm. "I'm sorry, but I can't accept that! You were on hand for both murders! Each time you had one of your spells! I covered up for you by hiding that knife, but I can't help you this time."

"I've killed nobody," Diana exclaimed, "and the Scorpio sign doesn't mean the killer has to be me. There are other Scorpios here, and anyone could leave that design to confuse us, whether they were a Scorpio or not!"

Carol shook her angrily. "Don't you realize how stupid that explanation is? Why not admit you had a fantasy? You could have done both murders during your mad blank spells. They can't punish you severely if you're mentally ill. At the worst, they'll put you away some-where for a few years."

Diana's eyes widened with panic and anger. "I'm not going to admit to things I didn't do and rot away in some insane asylum for the rest of my life. I want better than that!"

Carol released her and turned away. She shook her head. "I don't know what to do or say. How can I help you, when you're so clearly guilty?"

Diana wasn't too surprised at this lack of faith in her on Carol's part. It was about what she'd expected. That was why she'd been reluctant to have Barnabas send for her. There was going to be no support from her sister.

There was a knock on the room door. Carol opened it to let Dr. Meyer in. The usually austere man was now clearly badly upset.

Advancing to Diana with a grave expression, he said, "We are in most serious trouble now."

"Yes," she said in a small voice.

"You had another of your spells last night?"

"Yes."

He glanced toward Carol with some annoyance. "I would appreciate it if you'd leave me alone with your sister," he said.

Carol frowned. "I think I should remain."

"Why?" the doctor demanded.

"I want to protect Diana," Carol replied. "I don't want to see her blamed for something she didn't do."

Dr. Meyer arched his gray eyebrows. "I have no in-tention of blaming anyone for anything at this time. Your sister is my patient, and as her doctor I demand the right to talk to her privately."

Diana was baffled by this new diversion. The argument between the doctor and Carol was becoming a bitter one and seemed so pointless. She gave her sister an appealing look. "Please do what Dr. Meyer asks."

Carol still stood there defiantly. "He's probably going to use everything you say against you."

"I don't care," she told her. "Go. I'll see you later."

"If that is how you feel," Carol said coolly. "I'll be getting legal advice about our position here. Don't forget that Graham is visiting us today." With that, she wheeled around and strode out of the room.

When she had gone, the doctor gave his full attention to Diana again. "I must say you behaved wisely just now."

"I hope so."

He waved her to an easy chair by the dresser. As she sat down, he began to pace up and down worriedly before her. With a sigh, he said, "Now let us try to get your story."

"Where will I begin?" she asked.

He halted in front of her. "From the time you first woke up last night? From the moment you felt the black-out coming on."

She sensed that he was linking the two moments and knew this was wrong. She also was aware that this simplification could indicate he was judging her before she told her account of the night's happenings, that he already considered her responsible for the murder of Dr. Decker.

So she said, "I was wakened by an intruder in this room. We have no means of protection, since you allow no locks on the doors."

He frowned. "A necessary rule. Please go on."

"A phantom figure came to me in the darkness, and I was choked by someone with skeleton-like hands."

Dr. Meyer's gray eyes were suspicious. "No doubt this was a dream, a kind of delirium."

"No," she said sharply. "It really happened. I fainted, and when I came to, I went out to the hall to call for help. The light had burned out, and it was hard to see anything. I was frantic."

"Go on," the doctor said stiffly.

"Next I saw Dr. Decker on the stairs. It was then the cloaked figure came out of the shadows again and hurled him back down the stairway. I heard his scream and blacked out. I don't remember anything else until I came to in the garden."

He was looking at her with pity and concern, but there was nothing in that stern, lined face to suggest he believed any detail of her story.

"You apparently were in blackout for a long period," he said.

"Yes."

His shrewd eyes were searching her face. "This phantom you claim you saw. Can you describe it?"

"Only that it wore a hood and a flowing cape."

"Would you say it was a man or a woman?"

"I don't know." She had the feeling he was backing her into a kind of corner.

"Your description rather suggests the figure of the Lost Lady of Turnbridge. I know you've heard the legend— that she appears to warn of approaching death."

"Yes," she said with resignation. "It's typical of other legends of the same type. A ghost is often said to materialize and announce impending death."

"Just so," Dr. Meyer observed. "I believe Collinwood has a similar legend. Only in that case, it had to do with drowning and the appearance of a Phantom Mariner."

"I've been told about it," she said.

"It could be possible," he said smoothly, "that you have been listening too much to these stories and they have etched themselves on your imagination, even to the extent of your thinking you have seen the phantom."

She now saw what he'd been leading to. "No," she protested, "that's not the case. All that I've told you happened."

He sighed. "It is difficult to credit."

"I'm sorry." She saw that the warning Barnabas had given her had been well founded.

"So am I," he said. "This could have severe consequences for the clinic. Under other circumstances, I would be inclined to think you were merely the victim of a bad dream and one of your blackouts, and that Dr. Decker had accidently fallen on the stairs and killed himself. But to complicate things, there is the business of the Scorpio design, the same thing that we discovered on Hope Fenway's forehead. That suggests deliberate murder and the desire of the murderer to leave a calling card."

"I wonder . . ." she said.

He gave her a penetrating look. "It has to be that or the unlikely alternative that one of our patients had come upon both bodies and made the crude drawing."

"Without having been the killer?" she said.

"Yes." He paused. "You have said you are a Scorpio."

"And so have you," she reminded him quietly.

He looked uncomfortable. "I hope I may be ruled out of all this. There are two other Scorpios among our patients, Paul Miles and Dawn Walsh."

Both names had a special meaning for her. She said, "Dawn Walsh came to my room earlier last night. I had trouble getting her to leave."

"Oh?"

"Yes. She seemed very confused."

"The strain of recent events has made her condition worse," the doctor agreed.

"And when I came out of my blank spell in the garden, I was confronted by Paul Miles. He was wandering out there at dawn. He seized me roughly and talked in a strange manner. I might have had more trouble with him if Barnabas hadn't come along and scared him away."

"Barnabas mentioned the incident to me," Dr. Meyer said. "Miles can be frightening. As soon as this trouble is settled, I will have him sent away from here—unless we find him guilty of the murders, in which case the police will take responsibility for him."

"Then you do consider him a suspect?"

"Probably our prime suspect," Dr. Meyer said frankly. "But at this point it is hard to be sure. Your own story is puzzling, as you must realize."

"I've told the truth," she said in a low voice.

"As you see it," he replied dryly. This could only mean that he was accepting her testimony as that of an insane person. He didn't think she was a reliable witness.

"What happens next?" Diana asked.

"The police will be here soon," Dr. Meyer said unhappily. "There will be the usual investigation, and I suspect you may have a lot of questions put to you."

"I understand."

"Barnabas Collins also has some explaining to do," the doctor continued. "I have given him permission to come and go as he likes, but there is a rule that even patients with such privileges are to be back at Turnbridge House at ten. He violated that rule."

"I'm sure he must have had a good reason."

"There can be no reason for such a breach of the clinic rules," Dr. Meyer said with some anger. "But that is another matter. You need not remain in your room. You may come downstairs whenever you like."

"Thank you," she said.

The gray-haired doctor hesitated. "And don't let the police put words in your mouth. If you feel the questioning too arduous, please let me know and I will do all I can to assist you."

"I will," she promised, grateful for this small offer of assistance. At least it meant she wasn't being entirely deserted by him.

"You should be warned your position is precarious," he said.

"But I'm not in any way responsible!"

"The police are the ones who will decide that," he pointed out.

"I know."

"Try and rest as much as possible." He sighed. "We're going to miss Dr. Decker here."

"I know," she agreed.

"Still, we must not brood about that now. The important thing is to discover his murderer. I'm sure you feel the same way."

"I do. I wish there was some sort of lock for our rooms at night."

He looked annoyed. "You brought that up before."

"I no longer feel safe here."

"The arrangement is for your good," he told her. "In the future, it would seem, we must have a night guard or nurse. At least until the murders have been solved."

"A guard can't watch all the rooms at the same time," she protested.

"I'm sure it will offer adequate protection," he said with some annoyance. "But that is something to think of later. Just now I'm expecting the police momentarily." He gave her a curt nod and went out.

Dr. Meyer left her with the uneasy feeling that he was of the opinion the others needed protection from her more than she did from them. Although he had let her know there were other suspects, she was worried that he considered her the most likely one. She had an overwhelming desire to talk with Barnabas again.

Not knowing what the situation was on the front stairway, she took the rear steps down to the ground floor. Then she made her way to the dining room to have some coffee and toast. When she went into the big dark room, she saw Dr. Nils Ayler by the sideboard pouring himself a cup of the hot liquid. His cup filled, he glanced around at her with a surprised expression.

"I didn't expect you down here," he said.

"No?"

"No," he said. "Not after what I heard from Dr. Meyer."

"I don't follow you," she said, uneasy under his grim study.

"It oughtn't to be all that hard," he said. "Dr. Decker is dead, and you suffered another of your spells last night. I would expect you to be kept in your room, at least until the police arrive."

"Dr. Meyer gave me permission to come down here," she said.

The young doctor gave her a derisive look. "I'd call that a grave mistake," he said.

His attitude aroused her anger. "Are you saying you think I'm the one to be blamed for what happened to Dr. Decker?"

"Since you ask me directly, yes, I do," Dr. Ayler told her coolly.

CHAPTER NINE

Anger flooded through her, and she felt faint. She knew she could not remain in the same room with the cruel young man she'd come to hate so. She abruptly rushed by him and out to the reception hall. Not until she was a distance away from the dining room did she pause and lean weakly against the wall.

"Diana, what are you doing down here?" It was the voice of Barnabas at her elbow.

She looked up at him wearily. "I came down for coffee. Dr. Ayler was in the dining room. He taunted me about the murders."

"That doesn't surprise me," he replied.

"Let's get away from the house," she begged him.

"We daren't go far," he said. "The police will want to talk to all of us when they get here."

"Can't we safely go to the gardens?"

"Yes. We can tell from there when their cars arrive," Barnabas said. His deep-set eyes were fixed on her worriedly. "Do you feel up to it?"

"I have to talk with you."

He said, "I'll take you out there and then I'll return and get some coffee. We can have it out there in the sun. It will be an improvement over that gloomy dining room."

He escorted her out to one of the wooden benches a distance from the mansion but still within sight of the driveway. The sun was strong, and it was comfortably warm. Diana waited there while Barnabas went back to the dining room. She closed her eyes and tried to calm herself. The events of the night had left her in a nearly exhausted state. Her main fear was that this weariness might be the cause of her having still another blackout. She certainly couldn't afford that with the police coming and the necessity of keeping a clear head to give an account of last night.

The sound of footsteps on the gravel walk made her open her eyes, and she saw that Barnabas had returned with a tray containing two cups of coffee and a plate of toast. He placed it on the bench between them and sat with her.

"Drink the coffee," he said. "It will help. And try some of the toast."

"I will," she said taking up a cup.

Barnabas held one of the steaming cups in his hand. "Everyone is awake now. There's plenty of talk going on in there about what happened."

She sipped her coffee. "I'm sure of that."

"Poor old Decker," he said. "He was the best of the lot."

"I agree."

"He never was able to reconcile his conscience after what he did back in Germany," Barnabas went on. "But I think he honestly tried to make up for his past."

"That's what I felt," she said.

"Dr. Meyer will find him difficult to replace," Barnabas said. "I hope he doesn't make the same mistake he made with Dr. Ayler."

The hot coffee was making her feel better, but she still didn't want any of the toast. "I agree that Dr. Ayler is a hateful bully."

"He is more than that," Barnabas said with a significant glance for her. "He is an impostor."

This came as a startling revelation. She stared at the handsome Britisher. "What do you mean?"

"Exactly what I've told you. Ayler is an impostor. He is here under false pretences."

"You mean there is no Dr. Ayler?"

He smiled bleakly. "There was a Dr. Ayler, all right. And he did have a practice in Hollywood. He left there when our Ayler claims he did. But there are discrepancies between the rest of the facts and what our bald-headed friend claims."

"Go on," she said excitedly.

Barnabas glanced toward the house and then at her again. He spoke in a low, tense voice, saying. "None of this must be repeated. I'm not ready to bring this out in the open yet. So I must have your word you'll consider this a strict confidence."

"You can depend on me."

"I know that," he said. "But with police questioning and all the rest ahead, I wanted to make the facts plain. The real Dr. Ayler left Hollywood and went to Hawaii. He is still there. He did not come East."

"Could there be two Dr. Aylers?"

Barnabas shook his head. "I've been giving a lot of time to digging up these facts. The long distance calls at Collinwood will be staggering this month, but I'm sure it will be worth it. There is only one Dr. Nils Ayler listed with the American Medical Association."

Diana was stunned. While she had always disliked the cruel shaven-headed young man, she had never dreamed that he might not be a doctor or that he was here under an assumed identity. He had surely played his role of a medical man well.

"How could Dr. Meyer make the mistake of hiring him?" she asked.

Barnabas finished his coffee and put the cup down. "Probably the pressure of things here didn't give him a chance to properly check on Ayler's credentials."

"But who can he be?"

"That is a most interesting point," Barnabas said, taking a look in the direction of the old mansion again.

"Have you told all this to Dr. Meyer?"

"Not yet. I only confirmed some of the facts last night," Barnabas told her.

"You'll have to tell him," she said earnestly.

He nodded. "I know that, and I will, as soon as I get the opportunity. What is holding me back is waiting for the police. And then I may have difficulty getting Dr. Meyer to listen to me."

"Why?"

"I'm under the same dark shadow as yourself," he pointed out. "I am registered here as a mental case."

"I'd forgotten," she admitted.

"That's easier for us than it is for others."

"But there is nothing wrong with you now," she protested, "so there is no reason why your word should be doubted. Whatever neurosis you had has been cured."

"I'd like to think so," Barnabas agreed, "but I still haven't gotten a clean bill of health from Dr. Meyer. And he will have to give it to me. Technically, I'm also answerable to Dr. Ayler and can be judged by him."

She felt alarm at his words. "But that isn't right. You know that he's not a doctor and he's here under an assumed name."

"I still have to convince Dr. Meyer of that," Barnabas cautioned her. "That could take time. If I went directly to him at this moment and burst out with the story, he'd probably have me confined to a solitary cell without even bothering to check on Dr. Ayler, and while I was being treated as violently insane, Ayler would be carrying on as before."

"I hadn't thought of that."

"I have to wait until I can get Dr. Meyer to make the proper phone calls and get in touch with the right people," Barnabas said. "That's why the information has to be kept secret for a little time."

Her eyes were wide. "Could he be the murderer?"

Barnabas sighed. "I've been asking myself that."

"What do you think?"

"He could be," Barnabas said, "and if not, he might be mixed up in the crimes in some other way."

"He seems to especially hate me," she said.

"I've noticed that," Barnabas agreed. "He's as un-balanced as any of the patients here. It is possible that either Dawn Walsh or Paul Miles could be the murderer. But if either of them is guilty, I'd be willing to bet he knows about it."

"How can you find out the truth?"

"Maybe the police will do that," Barnabas said. "My own theory about Ayler is so far out that it rivals your story of the phantom—and you can be sure Dr. Meyer considers that a fantasy on your part."

"But it isn't!" she complained.

"Don't forget you are a mental patient," he said with a wry look. "You aren't judged by normal standards. It's the same with me. You remember the night you saw that monster animal with the amber eyes?"

"I'm not likely to forget it."

"You had an idea it might be a werewolf. I scoffed at what you said."

"Yes."

He sighed. "I owe you an apology. I think I was wrong."

"Wrong?" she gasped.

"Yes," Barnabas told her grimly. "I think you did see a werewolf, and there is only one explanation for that. Quentin Collins is back in the area. As usual, in some disguise."

"Quentin Collins?" she said.

"He's the one who has caused the trouble before. And it seems we have had him here under our noses. The shaven head threw me off the track, but give him dark

110

hair and sideburns, and I'm sure the features of Dr. Ayler would match those of Quentin."

Diana was astounded. She wanted to ask him a host of questions but there was no chance. For at that moment the police cars arrived with a screeching of tires in front of the main entrance of Turnbridge House. It was time for her and Barnabas to go in for questioning with the others. He gave her a reassuring look and then taking her by the arm guided her toward the house.

This investigation was much more thorough and disrupting than the previous one. Because Dr. Decker had been the murder victim, and Dr. Meyer was overloaded with responsibility, Dr. Ayler took charge of a great deal of the activity. It was he who arranged for the staff and patients to be interviewed by the police in turn, and when the interviews were over, he was on hand to assign them to other tasks. To Diana it was a mad situation, knowing, as she did, that the cold, efficient doctor was in reality a fake.

Her turn to be interviewed by the Police Inspector came fairly early. She could tell by his manner that he had heard a full account of her ramblings the previous night, but he asked her to go over it again while a younger officer took it all down on a tape recorder.

When she'd finished, the Inspector studied her closely. "That's a very strange story, Miss Collins," he said.

"There surely have been stranger ones," she replied. "I can vouch that it is true."

The Inspector shifted in his chair. "I'm trying to be considerate of you, Miss Collins. This is a mental hospital, and you are a patient. Are you asking me to accept your account of this phantom as fact?"

"Yes."

"It's asking a lot," he said dryly.

"I could have kept silent," she said. "That way I wouldn't have been involved."

He took a moment to consider this before he said, "That's quite true. But since you are a mental case, it's not likely you'd do the wise thing, even though you might realize what it was."

She gave him a reproving look. "Must one be mad to decide on an honest course?"

111

He crimsoned. "I didn't mean that the way it sounded," he said. "If you stopped insisting that you saw Decker shoved to his death, I'd be inclined to accept this as an accident—an accident which happened freakily after a murder. There are such coincidences."

"I'm sorry to spoil your theory," she said.

"The Scorpio lipstick drawing is surely the work of one of the inmates here," the Inspector went on. "But that was done after Dr. Decker's death. I don't think it has to mean the one who did it is anything but demented. It needn't indicate the person was a murderer."

"I see," she said. "So it's only my story you have to go on."

"And it's not much," the Inspector said with resignation. "Even you have to admit that."

"It was vivid enough to send me into a blackout."

"The blackout might have come first, and then you imagined the other," the officer said. "You might even be the one who drew those Scorpio signs on the girl's head and on Decker's."

"Because I'm a Scorpio?"

He nodded. "A Scorpio and a mental patient."

She smiled bitterly. "That part of being a mental patient seems to make anything possible."

"I'm trying to keep an open mind," he protested.

"I wonder," she said. "Or do you see us all as a group of mad people whose words and actions can't be accounted for?"

He smiled at her bleakly. "I'm trying to see you as you are. And that is not as easy as you'd think. You have one person in your group who backs you up strongly. I guess I needn't say that it's Barnabas Collins."

"Barnabas found me in the garden," she said.

"Yes. He seems to feel you're telling the truth. But then, he isn't exactly a reliable witness. He's a patient here, and in the past he had some nasty trouble with the local authorities. You're probably aware that for years he harbored the delusion that he was tainted by a vampire curse. He roamed the countryside at night and had half the local people believing he was some kind of living dead person."

"He is ready to admit all that," she said, "and the fact that he is here as a patient shows that he wants to be cured. In fact, I'd say he was perfectly normal."

"Maybe," the Inspector said. "But he was out roaming again last night. Neither Dr. Ayler nor I consider that a healthy sign. He could be reverting to his former madness."

Diana couldn't tell whether the Inspector was baiting her or not, but his mention of Dr. Ayler upset her. She wished she could answer by informing the smug police officer Ayler was a faker. Instead, she had to content herself by saying quietly, "If you think him mad, you are very wrong."

"We won't argue," the Inspector said. "Your sister also has done her best to defend you. But I can tell she is as worried about your mental state as I am. I understand Dr. Decker was a favorite of yours?"

"Yes. I liked him."

"What has happened must be distressing to you."

"It is."

He nodded. "Well, that is all for now. If you should decide that that phantom business was all in your mind, I won't be angry. You can get in touch with me at any time. I'll always be glad to hear amended testimony from you. I accept that you are still not well."

His dismissal of her was another humiliation. He all but suggested that she was insane to the point where her testimony wasn't really worth anything. She had the frightening feeling that he would take this stand. She had sensed that her story of the phantom would be ignored and he would put the death of the elderly doctor down to an accident. He had strongly hinted at this during the interview. There was one saving point: she wouldn't be considered a murderess.

Dr. Nils Ayler was waiting for her in the hallway. "You've finished in there?"

"Yes."

"Then go to your room," he ordered. "Your sister feels you need rest. I understand you have a visitor coming later today."

"I'm not sure I feel well enough to see anyone," she told him.

His cruel face showed no expression. "I'll leave that to Carol. She can best decide for you."

"Why?" she demanded. "I'm not incapable of knowing my own mind."

"You are a patient here, and you will do as I say," he sternly ordered.

She hesitated and then went to the stairway and up to the third floor. Let him flaunt his authority if he liked. He wouldn't have long to do it if Barnabas was able to expose him as he'd planned. She walked down the hallway to her own room and went inside. Exhausted, she stretched out on the bed and almost at once sank into a deep sleep.

Carol woke her by coming into the room. She was dressed in a pale-blue suit which accentuated her blondness. It was evident she had gone to some trouble to look her best for Graham Weeds.

Coming over to the bedside, she said, "Graham is here. He's waiting in my room to see you."

She sat up. "I'm not well. I'd rather not talk to him."

Carol looked angry. "You're just trying to be difficult."

"No," she protested. "You know what we've all been through here today."

"And you knew Graham was coming."

"I have nothing to say to him. He has come to see you. Why bring me into it?"

Carol stood there. "Because I want him to see how you are. He is our legal adviser, and I want him to have an idea of your condition. Of your improvement."

Diana got up from the bed with a bitter smile. "I wouldn't say there was any."

"You've got to see Graham!" her sister said. "Otherwise, he'll blame it on me."

Reluctantly she freshened up and put on another dress, then went to Carol's room. Her sister and the young lawyer were waiting for her. He came to greet her, a sandy-haired, weakly good-looking young man whose eyes were set too narrow in his thin face.

"Diana!" he said warmly. "I was afraid I wasn't going to see you." He politely kissed her cheek. Not the warm

114

lover's kiss he'd offered her so many times before he'd turned to Carol.

"A lot has been happening here," she said.

"I know," he said, his brow furrowing. "Carol has been telling me."

"I mentioned that you've been seeing a phantom," Carol said in a taunting voice. "But the police apparently aren't impressed. I hear they've decided Dr. Decker's death was accidental."

"I'm not surprised," Diana said quietly. Things were working out about as she had expected.

Graham Weeds was looking at her. "Of course, the girl was murdered."

"Yes," she said.

"And those strange astrology signs were lipsticked on both her forehead and Dr. Decker's?"

"The Scorpio sign," Diana said mockingly. "You know that's my sign. Do you think I did it?"

His thin face flushed. "What gave you that idea?"

Standing in the background, Carol spoke, "She's full of aggressive tendencies. Dr. Ayler thinks she is in no way responsible for what she says or does."

Diana tried hard to control her rage. "I see your time catering to Dr. Ayler hasn't been wasted." Turning to Graham she added. "You should see them together. Very romantic!"

Carol crossed to her angrily. "If you weren't insane, I wouldn't let you get away with saying that."

"I feel very sane at this moment," she told her.

Carol smiled jeeringly. "That's what I'd expect you to say."

Graham Weeds looked concerned. "Please don't quarrel. I don't want that. And, Diana, try and take advantage of being here. Do what you are told and see if you can't soon recover from this breakdown you've had."

She stared at him directly. "Do you really want that?"

"Certainly I do," he said, seeming startled. "What would make you doubt it?"

"I don't know," she said softly. "I don't really know."

"If there's anything you want," he said, awkwardly, "anything I can have sent here, please let me know. Just

115

try to keep out of all this trouble that is going on. I'd stay strictly to myself if I were you."

"She'd be better avoiding the company of Barnabas Collins," Carol commented.

"Barnabas Collins?" the lawyer repeated the name as a question.

"Yes," Carol said with a malicious smile. "He's another patient with almost as many demented ideas as Diana. She's always with him."

Graham Weeds showed worry. "As I said before, Diana, it might be best to avoid the company of other patients, especially considering what has been happening."

"Thank you for your concern," she said. "Is that all?"

He made a feeble gesture with his right hand. "All except that it is good seeing you again, Diana."

"Goodbye, Graham," she said. And she turned and quickly left the room. She could imagine Carol ridiculing her after she went. It seemed her sister couldn't make her small enough in the lawyer's eyes. She never ceased attempting to belittle her in front of him. This hospital for the insane made a perfect background for her efforts in that direction.

The interview left Diana in a defiant mood, and instead of going back to her room as Dr. Ayler had ordered, she went downstairs. She wandered to the library where Hope Fenway had once acted as librarian. The room had no windows, and so was in darkness. She switched on the light and went inside.

There, standing with a frightened expression on her lovely face was the former model, Dawn Walsh. She backed up fearfully on seeing Diana.

"I'm not doing anything wrong," she protested.

Diana stared at her. "I didn't say you were."

"I came here to try and talk to her," Dawn said earnestly.

"To who?"

"Hope. This was her room, where she used to be. I thought she'd tell me who killed her."

Diana wondered about the girl. Was she as frightened as she really pretended? Or was this a sly way of covering up for something? It was hard to say. She could understand the uneasiness outsiders showed in dealing with mental patients. It was hard to read what the insane were thinking.

She said, "You can't really believe that Hope would talk to you from the other side of the grave?"

Dawn nodded in a frightened fashion. "I've come in here before, and I've heard her voice... I hear voices of the dead all the time."

"I doubt that," she said quietly.

"You think they won't talk to me because I'm so ugly," the other girl said.

"No. I don't think anything of the sort."

"You do!" Dawn said pitifully. "People hate to look at my face. That is why I have to stay in the dark."

"That's all wrong!" she protested.

Dawn was smiling triumphantly. "But I see things in the darkness that no one else does."

"You must get over the feeling you are ugly," Diana told her.

"I *am* ugly!" She said, raising her hands to her face. "The scars are too deep. They can't fix them!"

"They have fixed them," Diana argued with her. "You're better-looking than most girls."

"You're lying!"

"No." It was a strange dilemma Diana found herself in in this isolated room trying to reason with the demented girl. It was useless. Dawn wouldn't listen to her. She decided to try to change the subject to something else. She said, "Why don't you read a book? The room is filled with them."

"I don't like to read!" Dawn said in a sulky voice.

"It would be good for you."

A crafty smile crossed her face. "Do they have any books about werewolves?"

"Werewolves?" Diana repeated sharply. "What made you ask that?"

"Don't you know?" Dawn taunted her.

"If I did, I wouldn't be asking you," Diana told her.

The mad girl's smile was sly. "You know!"

Diana was sure the other girl had seen the same monster she'd met on the grounds. Buried in her twisted mind was a memory of the same yellowish-gray creature with the slavering jaws that had tried to attack Diana.

She said, "Tell me where you saw the werewolf!"

Dawn repeated, "The werewolf?" At the same time, an expression of terror crossed her face.

"What about the werewolf?" the question was asked in a harsh voice. Diana whirled around to look into the livid face of Nils Ayler.

"Nothing," she said.

"I know better," the doctor snapped. He glared at the terrified Dawn Walsh. "Where did you hear about this werewolf?"

"She was telling me about it," Dawn quivered.

Dr. Ayler turned on Diana. "So that's it," he said harshly. "You're entertaining yourself by filling this poor demented creature's head with wild lies!"

"That's not true!" she protested.

His cruel eyes blazed at her. "Didn't I give you orders to remain in your room?"

"I don't remember!"

"I think you do," he snapped. "We have a way of dealing with patients who refuse to do as they are told." With that, he seized her roughly by the arm.

"Let me go!" she cried, clawing at him with her free hand.

The vicious doctor quickly got hold of that hand, as well, and propelled her from the room as Dawn stared at them with agonized eyes.

Diana continued to struggle against him, but it was no use. He was dragging her down the dark hallway toward the cellar steps. And she knew only too well what awaited her down there—the shadowy horror of the violent cells!

CHAPTER TEN

All Diana's protests and struggles were proving useless. Dr. Nils Ayler was strong and agile. He soon had reached the steep cellar stairs and forced her down to the damp, dark regions. Her fear grew as they went the length of the gloomy place and she found herself in the area known as the violent ward once again. Managing to control her with one hand, he used the other to open the door of one of the cells and flung her inside.

As he snapped the bolt on the cell door, he glowered at her through the barred opening. "Maybe this will teach you a lesson!"

"Don't you dare leave me here!" she cried.

His cruel face showed a smile. "You'll have plenty of time to calm down."

"Wait until Dr. Meyer hears about this!" she sobbed.

"Dr. Meyer will congratulate me for what I've done," he said. "You are a trouble-maker, deliberately upsetting the other patients."

"That's not so!"

The shaven-headed impostor who chose to call himself Dr. Ayler seemed extremely sure of himself. Was Barnabas right about him? Was he really the renegade Quentin back in this disguise? And was it he she'd seen transformed into a snarling werewolf?

He gave her a final sneering look. "Perhaps by the time I return you'll have learned better manners."

"You had no right to treat me this way," she stormed.

"Mental patients are subject to the discipline of their doctors," he reminded her with a mocking smile. "I find you need disciplinary treatment, so I'm giving it to you. No one is going to interfere. You'd be wise to make up your mind to that."

"We'll see," she said.

He made no reply, but vanished from the barred opening. She heard his footsteps retreating on the stone of the corridor as he left her alone and a prisoner. All the energy seemed to drain out of her, and she slumped on the cold stone floor with her face in her hands. Gently she sobbed.

She'd been dragged to this awful place by a man who was probably an impostor. It was too frustrating. No doubt Barnabas was on the point of unmasking the fake Dr. Ayler, and yet it was her bad luck to fall victim to him before it happened. What cruelty would he wreak on her next? What would be his new move to humiliate her and undermine her mental health?

There was now no doubt this place would take a toll of her already tormented nerves. Was it his purpose to drive her completely mad? Did he hate her that much? And if so, why? He seemed to be friendly with her sister, Carol, and yet from the start he'd shown a dislike of her. It was a puzzle, and she had no idea of its solution.

Dr. Decker's death was being listed as an accident. But she knew better. The old doctor had vaguely suggested he knew who Hope Fenway's murderer was and had appeared almost ready to tell her the name of the guilty party. But he'd been eliminated before he had a chance to name the murderer. Diana began to wonder if Dr. Ayler might not be the culprit.

Dawn Walsh had seemed to know more than she told about the werewolf business. Had the demented girl been merely bragging, or did she have some new information about the supernatural demon haunting the area? Whatever the case, Dr. Ayler had been quick enough to literally drag her away from the terrified girl.

Now Diana was a prisoner again in this place reserved for the violently insane. Would it be long before she had a chance to plead her case? When would Barnabas or Dr. Meyer note her absence and come to her rescue? She was sure Carol would not aid her in this instance. The wily Dr. Ayler would tell her some smooth story to win her over to his side, and Carol would be pleased enough to believe the worst about her. Her only chance for freedom depended on Barnabas or the senior doctor.

Hours passed. Dinnertime arrived, and there was nothing sent down to her. She was hungry and thirsty. Her uneasiness returning, she started to pace in the long, narrow cell. Moving back and forth slowly, she racked her brain for some way of getting word to the others. It seemed hopeless.

The only light available in the dark cell came from a tiny light in the ceiling of the corridor. Its weak glow came in through the opening in the cell door. She moved close to the door, and grasping the bars, drew herself up to them and gazed vainly down the length of the shadowed corridor. There was no one out there.

She was tempted to scream, but decided it would merely be a useless waste of energy. So she waited. Dinnertime passed, and then it was mid-evening, and after that late night. Outside, the darkness would have fallen, and she would have been missing for hours. It was incredible that no one had noticed.

The gloom in the cellar was unrelenting. As evening gave way to night, she began to experience new fears. Would she be subjected to a visit by the phantom again? It was a frightening possibility, and one she didn't dare dwell on.

She was standing by the barred opening when she heard the shuffle of stealthy footsteps. At once she knew they had a sinister message for her. Swallowing hard, she stepped back from the opening and waited in the shadows of the cell for what would happen next. The shuffling footsteps came nearer until at last they halted by her door. As yet she seen no one!

But she could hear a nervous, labored breathing from out there. It was a macabre sound already familiar to her. She'd heard it when she'd encountered the eerie Lost Lady of Turnbridge before. Was the phantom here to warn she was the next to die? Diana waited with a numbing fear taking hold of her.

There was a rustling sound, and then a hand groped up and bony fingers circled one of the bars. Diana took another step away from the door and watched with wide, terrified eyes.

"Diana!" her name was spoken by the unseen phantom in a hoarse whisper.

"Who is it?" she demanded in a small, frightened voice.

"You will die!" the voice was all too clear.

"No!"

"That is what I say!"

"Who are you? Why have you come here to torment me?" she cried.

She was answered by a mocking silence. The bony fingers vanished from the cell bars, and then she heard the shuffling footsteps moving away down the shadowed corridor. She rushed at once to the door, and seizing the bars, pressed herself against them to try to see out. But all she managed was a glimpse of a twisted moving shadow on the opposite wall of the long hall. Exasperated and discouraged, she let herself down with a tiny moan.

To all intents the phantom had come to her again. But this time she'd not seen it. Had this really been a visit from a ghost, or was someone playing a macabre trick on her? Since she was Ayler's prisoner down here, without anyone else knowing, the chances were all against its being a cruel joke. The visitation had meant something. No doubt she'd discover its meaning soon enough.

Weak from fear and lack of food and drink, she leaned against one of the whitewashed cement walls. What next? That was the nagging question now. Her head was aching in an old, familiar way, and she began to worry that another blackout might hit her.

If she suffered another loss of memory while she was alone down here, it was frightening to consider what the result might be. The phantom had whispered that she was going to die, and this began to seem all too likely. More and more she was convinced that the fake Dr. Ayler was the murderer and he feared she knew his secret. Therefore she was marked for death.

The crisis would surely come soon. Weakly she lowered herself to the floor again and tried to rest herself a little in a far corner of the cell. It was cold and uncomfortable, but she knew she should try to conserve her energy. She closed her eyes and attempted to relax.

In a few moments she dropped off into an uneasy sleep. She was at once plagued by Dr. Nils Ayler in a nightmare. The bald man was standing over her with a knife in his hand.

Giving her one of his mocking grins, he said, "This time the Scorpio sign will be carved on your forehead. I'll do it with this knife after I've finished you with it!"

She gazed up at him in abject horror. "No! You mustn't! I'll tell them who you are! That you're Quentin Collins in disguise!"

He gloated as he brought the knife closer to her. "Do you think I care about that now, Cousin?"

"Don't call me your cousin!" she cried.

"That is what you are, like it or not!"

"I hate you!" she told him. "You're wicked! You took on the shape of a werewolf to frighten me and threaten poor Dawn Walsh."

The knife was in his hand and poised above her heart. "No more demented than you, my pretty cousin," he taunted her.

"Let me go!" she begged. "Put away that knife! It is you who must be mad!"

She saw the knife was coming down on her, and so she hastily hurled herself to one side to escape its blow. Ayler let out an oath and came after her again. At the same time, the cell door was being pounded on, and she heard the click of a bolt being drawn back. These sounds brought her out of her sick nightmare with a moan and a start.

"Diana!" It was the familiar voice of Barnabas coming to her from the open doorway of the cell.

"Barnabas!" she called out weakly.

At once he was inside the cell and lifting her from the floor. His arm around her, he asked, "How long have you been in this place?"

"Since late afternoon."

"You hear that, Doctor?" Barnabas inquired indignantly, and Diana realized he wasn't alone.

From the corridor Dr. Meyer said, "I'm astounded to think that Dr. Ayler would take such responsibility on himself. I'll reprimand him severely when I see him."

"I should hope so," Barnabas said as he led her out to the freedom of the corridor.

Dr. Meyer was regarding her anxiously. "What happened between you and Dr. Ayler that made him put you down here?"

She grimaced. "I was talking to Dawn Walsh in the library. She said something about a werewolf. He came in and overheard us, and he accused me of agitating her by bringing up the werewolf legend."

"And?" the doctor asked.

"He became insanely angry and dragged me down here," she said. "I tried to fight free of him, but it was useless."

"Are you listening, Doctor?" Barnabas said. "Ayler merely indulged in a vicious mood to punish this poor girl for nothing."

Dr. Meyer looked upset. "It is unfortunate. I can only hope that Dr. Ayler will be able to provide me with some satisfactory explanation for this rash action."

"I don't doubt that he will, Dr. Meyer," Barnabas said angrily. "In the meantime, this unhappy girl has been suffering an ordeal down here." He turned to her. "Did he have anyone bring you food or drink?"

"No."

The handsome face was dark with anger as he glanced at Dr. Meyer again. "This is typical of the cruelty of Dr. Ayler," he told him.

Dr. Meyer frowned. "I can't understand it."

"At least, now you know," Barnabas said. "I'll take Diana up to her room and see she gets something for her hunger and thirst."

"Please do that," the doctor begged. "I'm going to try to locate Dr. Ayler and speak to some of the nurses."

Barnabas still had his arm around her. "Do you feel well enough to make the stairs?"

"Yes. With you here, I'm not afraid any longer," she said weakly.

He helped her down the corridor. "I began inquiring for you as soon as I returned."

"Where were you?"

"That's another story," he said. "I'll tell you when we get up to your room." He guided her along the hallway on whose wall she had seen the deformed shadow of the phantom such a short time ago. The memory of it made her shudder again.

Barnabas saw her safely to her room and then brought her a tray of sandwiches and some milk. Her hunger had vanished, but she forced herself to take the milk and then nibble on the sandwiches until she gradually began to feel less nauseated and more her regular self.

Barnabas stood by with an anxious expression on his face. "How are you now?" he asked.

"Well enough to hear more from you," she said wanly.

"Sure you can't manage another half of a sandwich?"

"Positive," she said. "Did you see any sign of Carol?"

"No. I knocked on the door of her room, but there was no answer."

"She must be out somewhere," Diana said. "She sometimes takes the car and goes over to Collinwood."

"I know," he agreed.

"What about Dawn Walsh?" she asked.

"Same thing. She doesn't seem to be anywhere around."

Diana said, "She's probably hiding in the dark somewhere. That's part of her madness."

Barnabas looked grim. "I'm only too well aware of the demented ideas of my fellow inmates here," he said. "I also checked on Paul Miles, and he's in his room asleep. Or pretending to be."

"Probably asleep," she said. "He's under constant sedation since his recent flare-up."

Barnabas was frowning. "I assume that's what Ayler hoped would happen with you. That his cruelty in putting you down in that lonely place would cause you to explode into violent madness."

"Perhaps."

"Did you give him any hint that you suspected he was an impostor?"

She shook her head. "No. I was very careful."

"Good. I was afraid you might have forgotten, in your anger and despair."

"I was tempted," she said, "but I remembered what you said."

Barnabas came over to her and smiled. He tenderly touched her hair and then bent down to kiss her with great gentleness. "You are an unusual girl," he said. "If we weren't both unfortunates in this mad house, I'd be tempted to tell you I've fallen in love with you."

Her eyes met his dreamily. "Tell me, anyway."

"Not the time or place," he said. "There are still too many puzzles to solve."

"I hate the puzzles, and I hate everything about here—except you."

Barnabas regarded her with knowing eyes. "Surely you don't include Brian Dale in that? He's harmless enough and certainly fond of you."

A startled look crossed her face. "I'd forgotten all about him."

"I thought so," he said.

"I wonder where he is," she said. "Why he didn't notice I was missing?"

"I can't imagine," Barnabas said. "Unless he and Ayler are closer than we suspect."

"I don't see Brian as a friend of Ayler's," she said, worried. "There has to be some other explanation."

Barnabas said, "Maybe we should speak to Dr. Meyer about him."

"We should," she insisted.

They went downstairs and found the doctor in his office. He listened to their queries about Brian Dale and looked uneasy. "I'll speak to the nurse on the second floor," he said and picked up the phone. After a brief exchange with the nurse he put down the phone and came around the desk to them. His thin face looked strained. "Dale is in bed, apparently in some kind of coma!"

He hurried from the office and ran upstairs. Diana and Barnabas were at his heels. When they reached the playwright's room, they found him fully clothed on his bed in an unconscious state. His breathing came with a weird rattling sound, and his face was purple. An empty glass lay on the floor by the bed along with a bottle of white tablets, many of them spilled out on the rug. A shocked nurse stood by the foot of the bed.

Dr. Meyer took the situation in at once. "Dale has tried suicide again," he exclaimed. "We'll have to work fast if we're to save him!"

The next hour was one of suspense and uncertainty. Dr. Meyer took the unfortunate young man to the examining room and used a stomach pump and all the other emergency treatment needed to save his life. She and Barnabas waited anxiously.

126

Finally they were rewarded by a gray-faced and weary Dr. Meyer coming out of the examining room to inform them, "Dale is coming around. He's going to be all right."

"Thank goodness," Diana said with a sigh of relief.

Barnabas asked the doctor. "Do you know what happened? Have you had a chance to question him?"

"Only briefly," the senior doctor said. "I'll leave him alone with the nurse to rest for a little. Then I'll ask him more questions."

They were both on their feet facing the doctor, and Diana asked, "Did you learn anything at all?"

Dr. Meyer looked troubled. "He claims he didn't make another suicide attempt. That the pills he took were the ones given him. But they'd been tampered with and much stronger ones substituted. By the time he realized this, it was too late. He was already on the point of passing out."

There was a moment of stunned silence before Barnabas said. "If we hadn't missed him and reached him in time, we'd have had another murder here—one like Decker's, with all the suggestion of its being Dale's own doing. We'd have assumed he'd killed himself."

Dr. Meyer moistened his dry lips with his tongue. "I don't want to jump to rash conclusions. But it is possible."

"Possible!" Barnabas said. "It's almost a certainty."

"The young man is very mixed up and weak," the doctor protested. "I'll have to talk to him further and make a test of the pills."

Diana said, "But he has told you someone tried to cause his death by substituting stronger tablets than he normally took?"

"Yes," Dr. Meyer said with grim reluctance.

Barnabas said, "Miss Carol Collins is missing. Diana thinks she may have gone over to Collinwood. May I have the car to take Diana over there and see if we can find her?'

Dr. Meyer became his old austere self. "It is very late, and even though I have often given you many liberties, this is a most unusual request."

"It is a most unusual night, Doctor," Barnabas said knowingly.

The doctor cleared his throat. "I'm not so much opposed to your going as to your taking this young lady with you. It's against all my rules."

"The way she suffered in that solitary cell tonight was also against your rules, but it happened," Barnabas said. "I have an idea it might be important to get in touch with Diana's sister and have her come back here and keep Diana company."

Dr. Meyer still hesitated, then said, "Very well. But don't be long. You know where to get the keys to the station wagon."

"Yes, sir," Barnabas said. "We'll be back as quickly as we can."

He guided her out to the reception hall and after a moment when he left her to get the keys, they went out together. Not until they were in the station wagon and driving in the direction of Collinwood did he make any attempt to explain the night's happenings to her.

Then, as they drove through the darkness, he told her, "Meyer knows what I've discovered about Ayler."

"That Ayler is a faker?"

"Yes, and he's taken it pretty hard. We drove up to Bangor together, and he made some further phone calls and inquiries on his own. He hasn't gotten complete proof, but he has discovered enough to know Ayler is not a doctor and his name is not Ayler."

"That is why he was so willing to do what you asked and give you this car?" she said.

"Right," Barnabas went on. "I haven't let him in on the big secret yet—that Ayler is Quentin Collins. If I told him that and dragged in the werewolf story, I might wind up in that cell you just got out of."

She stared at him anxiously. "It is a fantastic story!"

He glanced at her. "I know it. But you'd better believe it!"

"It's easy for me," she said. "I saw the monster. It had to be supernatural! It was too horrible to be an ordinary animal, even a mad one!"

"Agreed," Barnabas said, watching the road ahead. "There's not a doubt in my mind that our man is Quentin and that he is back here allowing himself the form of a werewolf when he likes."

"Dr. Meyer will never believe it when you tell him."

"I know that, so I may not tell him."

"But you can't let Quentin remain posing as Ayler?" she worried.

"No. We'll get rid of Quentin some way when the time comes."

A sudden thought had come to her. She stared bleakly ahead at where the car lights pierced the blackness of the night, and said in an awed voice, "And Carol has been flirting with him outrageously! They could be together tonight. She doesn't even guess the danger she's in."

"I've been thinking about that," he agreed grimly.

She turned to him. "We'll have to warn her!"

"No," Barnabas said. "We can't do that. I wouldn't trust her to keep it to herself. She might tell Quentin, and the whole thing would blow up in our faces."

"But we can't allow her to expose herself to him without knowing the danger!"

Barnabas said, "We'll try to chaperone her as much as possible. That's why I'm making this drive tonight. If they're together, we'll try to part them on the pretext that you need her with you."

"He'll be livid when he hears that I was freed from the cell," she reminded him.

"I'm not going to worry about that," Barnabas said. "And by tomorrow Dr. Meyer may be ready to accuse him of being an impostor. At the very latest, in another day the situation will come to a head."

"Quentin will deny the accusation, I suppose," she said bitterly.

"Whether he denies it or not, the situation will be too hot for him to remain," Barnabas said confidently. "I think he'll simply walk out."

"We'll be rid of him that easily?"

"It's happened that way before," Barnabas assured her. "What we have to worry about is the harm he may do before he goes."

"He'll want to even the score, particularly with you," she said.

"That won't be anything particularly new, either. Collinwood is just ahead."

Diana saw the lights of the old mansion; some were

on on the ground floor at the front of the house, and several of the bedroom windows upstairs showed lights.

She said, "It's late. I hope Elizabeth doesn't think it's too strange, our arriving at this hour."

"We haven't time to make polite explanations," Barnabas said. "We had to come, and that's that. Later we can tell her more."

Diana strained for some sign of Carol's car. "I don't see the car."

"Neither do I," Barnabas agreed. "We'll go inside and speak to Elizabeth in any case. Then we'll decide what to do and where they might have gone."

Diana sighed. "It's been a dreadful day and night."

He brought the car to a halt. "Let's hope there won't be too many more like it."

"I couldn't stand it if there were."

He got out of the car and went around and opened her door for her. Then they went up to the front entrance of Collinwood and rang the bell. A moment later the door was answered by Elizabeth.

Giving them a look of mild amazement, she said, "This is a night for visitors. Carol and Dr. Ayler have just left. Won't you come in?"

They accepted her invitation and followed her into the living room. Barnabas told her, "We can only stay a few minutes. I've promised not to keep Diana away from the hospital long. Have you any idea where the doctor and Carol went?"

Elizabeth smiled. "They spoke of driving by the Blue Whale Tavern and then going back to the clinic."

Diana asked, "And they only left a little while ago?"

"That's right," Elizabeth said, as she gave her an admiring glance. "I must say you're looking better. In spite of all the trouble you've been having at the hospital, you've gained by being there."

"I hope so," she said.

Barnabas remained standing. "We must have Diana over some afternoon soon. I'm sure Dr. Meyer will allow it now. He also seems pleased with her progress."

"It would be very nice to have you here when you can enjoy the grounds," Elizabeth told her. "And the days for that will be getting fewer. When October ends, it is usually cold and bleak in this area of Maine."

They stayed and chatted with her a little longer and then said good night. When they were back in the station wagon, Barnabas said, "I don't think she realized we were under tension or that there is anything wrong about Ayler."

"It didn't seem so," she agreed.

He started the car, and there was a resigned expression on his handsome face. "I think we can assume Carol will be safe enough. They'll drop by the Blue Whale and then drive back to Turnbridge House. I see no point in our going to the village."

"Ayler might guess we were suspicious of him," she suggested.

"That's how I feel," Barnabas agreed.

"So perhaps we'd better go back ourselves."

"We will," Barnabas said. "But first I'd like to drive you over to what is known as the old house, the original Collinwood. I'd like you to see it, as long as you're over here. It's where I have lived when visiting the family."

"You didn't stay at the main house?" Diana asked with surprise.

"No," Barnabas said as they drove on. "I've always preferred the old house. My servant Hare is occupying it now. The chances are I'll return to it when I'm discharged from the hospital. There are some things there I think you should see."

There was a hint of something she did not understand in his quiet statement. A suggestion of the sinister and frightening. With a worried look on her attractive face she settled back against the car seat as they drove through the darkness toward the old house.

CHAPTER ELEVEN

She knew it was going to be a short drive, so she sat quietly not attempting any conversation. Barnabas was busy at the wheel. Her mind fairly raced with thoughts, and many troubling questions presented themselves to her. What did the pattern of violence at Turnbridge House mean? Had she in any way been involved with the murder of Hope Fenway? And had she any responsibility in the other incident when Dr. Decker died? She thought not, but it worried her. And now there was the attempt on Brian Dale's life to consider—an attempt that had been craftily designed to look like suicide!

All of it had to be part of some larger plan, and Diana vaguely felt she was linked to the weird happenings. Did they have something to do with the supernatural? She felt they had. She had seen the eerie wolf-like monster, and also the phantom Lost Lady of Turnbridge. And now Barnabas had discovered positive proof that Dr. Nils Ayler was an impostor and likely to be the black sheep of the Collins family, Quentin Collins.

Quentin had apparently taken a dislike for her, though he seemed to get on well enough with Carol. He probably had a part in the dark things that were going on at Turnbridge House. It was known that he usually caused trouble whenever he appeared. He had cast insinuations about Barnabas, but she was not prepared to believe that malicious gossip.

Barnabas broke into her reverie by bringing the car to a stop. "Here we are," he said, indicating a building on the left that was all in darkness.

She gazed out at the shadowy building with a small thrill of uneasiness. "It looks deserted," she said.

"Hare doesn't bother much with lights," he replied. "And he keeps the shutters closed, which also prevents us from seeing any room lights from the outside. Let's go in for a few minutes."

He let her out of the station wagon and walked with her to the steps of the ancient building. Then he knocked on the door, and they waited for someone to open it. At least several minutes passed before she heard heavy footsteps from inside. Then the door was opened a fraction, and an ugly, beard-stubbled face stared out at them.

Barnabas said, "It's all right, Hare. I want to show Miss Collins the house."

Hare's gruesome-looking face was dark with suspicion. He glared at her, but he stood back and opened the door the full way so they could enter.

"He is a mute," Barnabas told her, "and very eccentric. You mustn't mind his manners. He is devoted to me, and a competent employee." They went down a short hallway to a wide doorway opening on the living room. Candles were burning on the mantel over the living room's fireplace giving the big room with its antique furnishings a special air of charm.

"This is a lovely room," Diana said, taking it in with delight.

Barnabas smiled. "I have always had an affection for this house. I'm glad you approve."

She turned to him. "You reflect the charm of its atmosphere."

His deep-set eyes met hers. "The house is associated with me in a number of ways," he told her. "Let me show you some more of it."

He took one of the candles from the mantel and led her through the other rooms holding it high for light. Whether the flickering flame of the candle was responsible for the subdued charm with which every room seemed to be endowed was a question. Certainly the house had a personality. All the fear she'd first felt about it vanished.

They came to another hallway, and Barnabas opened a door and with the candle held high, casting a magic glow on his gaunt, noble face, said, "Now I want you to see the cellar. And particularly one room in the cellar."

133

It struck her there was a certain urgency in his tone, and she decided it was for the purpose of showing her this room he'd brought her to the old house. He grasped her arm and helped her down the stairs to the earthen floor of the ancient cellar.

"We'll have to walk the length of the house," he warned her. "I'll keep hold of your arm so you won't stumble over anything."

"The house is larger than it looks from the outside," she said as they made their way through the blackness with only the glow of the candle to help them. On either side of them there were vague shadows of stored furniture and other items. At last they came to a door.

Barnabas paused before it. "Whatever you see in here, you must not be frightened," he said.

She looked up at him. "Why should I be, as long as I have you to protect me?"

He smiled faintly. "Please keep that thought in mind."

He turned the door knob and opened the door. This time he led the way and she followed him into a medium-sized, damp room. They'd gone halfway across it before she saw the coffin set up in one corner of it and gasped.

Barnabas turned to her. "I warned you not to be upset."

"But that casket?" she said.

"Is empty and shouldn't scare you," Barnabas said, staring at it with a melancholy expression. "During my long years of illness, that was my bed in the daytime hours. I left it only at dusk and returned to it every dawn."

Her eyes were wide with amazement. She studied him and said, "So it is true. That when you were ill you believed yourself to be a vampire, one of the living dead?"

"Yes," he admitted with a sigh. "You know the story of the first Barnabas and the curse put upon him?"

"I know the story."

"I had the conviction the curse had descended to me," Barnabas said, "and so for years I lived the life of a vampire."

She stared up at him anxiously. "That was when you were mentally ill. You can't be blamed for that. You are cured now."

"I hope so," Barnabas said rather sadly.

"I know you are."

134

He smiled at her, a troubled smile. "Yet there will always be the lingering fear that the condition will return, that I might become ill in the same manner again."

"You won't!"

"I wonder," he said.

"Let me help you," she begged. "And you can be a marvelous aid to me. Together we'll fight for keeping our sanity! Why don't we get married, Barnabas?"

He stood there in the eerie room, the casket in the background, and a wistful expression crossed his gaunt face. "I can think of nothing I'd like better," he told her.

"Then let us!" she begged.

"I must think about it," he said, "weigh my prospects. I wouldn't want you to be chained to anyone as ill as I was."

Diana indicated the coffin and the room with a sweeping gesture. "Forget about this place," she said. "You need never come here again. I'm glad you told me about it, since now I know what I must fight to save you."

The deep-set eyes studied her with wonder. "You are willing to devote your life to me?"

"Yes."

Barnabas placed an arm around her and drew her close to him. She raised her lips for his kiss and in the warmth of his embrace forgot the macabre tone of their surroundings. All she had endured, the illness and the fears, seemed justified by her finding this charming man.

He gently released her and said, "Now we must hurry back to Turnbridge House. I have kept you out too long."

Diana was glowing with the new-found togetherness between herself and Barnabas. In this mood it was difficult to face a return to the ancient house where so many dreadful things had happened lately, but she knew they must do this if they were to be free to pursue their lives together. They must have Dr. Meyer's approval and his pronouncement that they were ready to leave Turnbridge House and build lives of their own.

During the drive back, Barnabas said, "The next hours will be critical ones. I expect Dr. Meyer will confront Ayler with what he's found out about him sometime before tomorrow night."

"And then what?" she asked.

"I don't know," he admitted. "It depends entirely on how strong a reaction there is on Ayler's part, or Quentin's, if you wish to call him by his right name."

"You're that certain he is Quentin?"

"Yes."

She sighed. "Do you think he had a part in Hope Fenway's murder?"

"I don't know," Barnabas said. "He may have—evil always follows him. But I can't think why he'd want to murder her."

"Perhaps she found out who he is."

"Perhaps."

"But if he did it, why should he leave the murder weapon in my room?" she wondered. "That made Carol positive I did it, and even now I can't definitely say that during my blackout I didn't commit the crime. I could have!"

He gave her a warning glance. "That's dangerous thinking on your part."

"I can't help worrying."

"Don't try to see everything clearly at this point," was his advice. "Let it gradually take on perspective."

She was later to realize how good this advice was. They reached Turnbridge House and went inside to discover Nils Ayler and Carol standing together in the reception hall. They had apparently gotten back only a few minutes ahead of them, and greeted them with surprised looks.

Carol demanded, "Where were you?"

"Barnabas took me over to Collinwood for a drive," she said with a hint of defiance.

Carol gave Barnabas an accusing glance. "You know she is not supposed to leave here?"

"I had the permission of Dr. Meyer," Barnabas said calmly.

The fake Dr. Ayler gave him a sharp glance. "I think you're lying. You are still a patient yourself, despite the fact that you have many privileges. I'd say this time you've overstepped your limits. I'll speak to Dr. Meyer."

Barnabas smiled grimly. "You'd be wasting your time. We were sent out to try to locate you two. An attempt was made on Brian Dale's life while you were out."

Dr. Ayler scowled. "What nonsense is this?"

Diana spoke up, "It's true. Someone substituted dangerous pills for the ones Brian is taking. If he hadn't been discovered in time, he would have died."

Carol looked shocked. "When did all this happen?"

"When you two were visiting Collinwood," Barnabas said calmly. "There is no need for you to be alarmed. The crisis has passed. You may as well go quietly to bed." He turned to her, "I'll see you safely to your doom, Diana."

They left the baffled two to go on upstairs. When they were a safe distance from them, she said in a low voice, "They seemed surprised, but I wonder if Dr. Ayler is as innocent as he pretended."

"I doubt it," Barnabas said in a dry voice. At her door he kissed her good night again and suggested she place a chair by her door. "If anyone tries to get in, you'll at least hear them and have some warning," he told her.

She did what he suggested, and the night passed without any further incident. The next morning was cold and gray. It had rained during the night, and now there was fog blocking out the view of the ocean and cloaking the grounds of Turnbridge House in a dense, wet mist.

As soon as she had had breakfast, she asked permission to visit Brian Dale and was given it. She went to the playwright's room and found him sitting up with some pillows propped behind him and the morning newspaper in his hands. Aside from being extremely pale, he looked very much himself.

"Well!" she said.

The young man looked embarrassed. "Don't blame me!"

"We might have, if you hadn't survived," she warned him.

"That upsets me," he admitted. "Just when I'm ready to believe I'm cured, I'm placed in a position where it looks as if I have the same old suicidal wish."

"It was meant to seem that way," she said solemnly.

He looked at her with some amazement. "Do you honestly think so? Dr. Meyer was in here this morning, and he says it was negligence on the part of the dispensing nurse. When she made me up a new vial of pills, she gave me the wrong ones."

Diana was at once wary. If Dr. Meyer had told the young man this, there was probably a good reason for his doing so. She said quickly, "I'm sure whatever the doctor told you is correct."

"Even so, it's not what you'd call comforting," Brian said. "She makes a stupid error, and everyone says Brian Dale tried it again and made it. I'll never want to take any more pills."

She smiled. "Maybe you won't need them."

The pleasant young man nodded earnestly. "I have an idea that may be true. I place a different value on my life knowing I could have lost it accidentally. I'm over that suicide bit!"

"Then, being treated by Dr. Meyer has done you good. Just as it has benefitted all of us," she said.

He was staring at her. "I can tell being here has helped you. You fairly radiate new confidence."

Diana smiled. "I feel it. Even on this miserable morning I can almost tell myself that I'll not allow my nerves to get beyond me again, that I won't have any more of those awful blackouts."

"Stay with that idea," he encouraged her.

"I will," she said. "It would seem that Dr. Meyer will soon be having a new set of patients. Barnabas is also ready to leave."

"He was never as ill as the rest of us," Brian said.

Her face shadowed. "I wouldn't make too quick a judgment about him. It's possible his condition was even worse than ours."

"Does it matter, as long as he's well again?"

"No," she said.

"The two I really feel sorry for are Dawn Walsh and Paul Miles," Brian said in a gloomy tone. "Dawn was in here a little while ago, and I think she's worse than she was."

"I know," Diana agreed.

"And Paul Miles is being drugged so that he probably can't tell day from night. It's the only way Dr. Meyer can curb his violence." He paused and then looked at her shrewdly. "I think either Dawn or Paul killed Hope Fenway, don't you?"

"I can't make up my mind," she said.

"It has to be one of them," he argued. "Drawing that Scorpio on Dr. Decker's head with a lipstick sounds more like the cunning kind of trick Dawn might indulge in, so she's my number-one suspect."

"You could be right," she agreed, remembering her talk with Dawn the previous day, and how it had led to her being locked in one of the violent cells.

Brian gave her a searching glance. "What are your plans when you leave here?"

"I'm not sure yet," she said. "A new kind of life, if I'm lucky."

"You deserve to be lucky," was his reply. "And what about your sister? I mean, this romance between her and Dr. Ayler."

She was startled. She'd not thought the friendship between Carol and the impostor had been so obvious to the others. She said, "I can't think she's serious about him."

"Why not?"

"She's engaged to Graham Weeds, the lawyer who looks after our estate."

"The one you were engaged to?"

She blushed. "That was some time ago."

"And he's going to marry Carol now?" Brian said.

"Yes."

"I wonder," Brian said. "Carol and Ayler are pretty close. Maybe she's changed her mind about your lawyer."

"I can't imagine it," she said. "It caused most of the trouble between us."

"I guess that was the start of your breakdown. That and your father's being killed in the plane crash. Isn't that so?"

"Father's death, mostly."

"If Carol decides to marry Ayler, will you go back with that lawyer?"

Diana protested, "She'll never marry Ayler, or even think of it."

"Don't be too sure," Brian said. "What concerns me is how you feel about that Graham?"

"I'm over that," she said firmly. "No matter what happens, I won't consider Graham romantically."

"There is only Barnabas, then?"

She stared at him in surprise. "What do you mean?"

"I'm ticking off my rivals," he said with good humor. "If Graham is out of the game, then I've only Barnabas

139

to worry about. I'd like you to be my wife. You must know that."

Diana was taken back by his frank outburst. With a nervous smile, she said, "I'd say you are allowing yourself to become far too excited. If I remain here, I'll have Dr. Meyer reproving me."

"I don't want you to leave," the young playwright said.

"I have to," she told him firmly as she went out.

Diana went back to her bedroom, since it was too damp and miserable to go out. She'd only been there a few minutes when Carol joined her in the room. Her sister was in one of her unpleasant moods.

Carol began by coming over to her and asking, "Where did you and that Barnabas go last night?"

"I thought I told you," she replied calmly. "We went to Collinwood."

"Why did he take you over there?"

"We were looking for you."

Carol lifted her chin. "What I do shouldn't concern you."

"I was worried about you," she said.

"You needn't have been," her sister said. "I was with Nils Ayler."

"That's why I was worried."

Her sister showed surprise. "What do you mean?"

"I don't like him."

"Only because he can see through you and your other mad friends so clearly," Carol said.

She studied her with concern. "You can't really believe he's all that wonderful! He's arrogant and cruel!"

"You surely have no right to judge him!" Carol snapped back.

"Why not?"

Her sister came close and bent down so her face was only a foot or so from hers and in a low, tense voice said, "You know why not! You're probably a murderess! I saved your skin by taking that knife and wiping the fingerprints from it and hiding it. And I kept silent when the police found it. Just as I said nothing about Dr. Decker's death, either. And it was probably you who pushed him down the stairs in one of your blackouts."

Diana went pale as she listened to the tirade. Drawing back in her chair she said, "You can't prove that I did anything!"

"I wonder if you'd like me to try?" Carol demanded with sarcasm.

Diana couldn't understand her sister's rage. She said, "Why should Dr. Ayler mean so much to you if you're going to marry Graham Weeds?"

"Who said that I was?" Carol demanded. And with an icy smile she turned and left the room.

Diana sat there stunned. It was too much. Clearly Carol was more unstable than she'd realized. In her own sickness she'd not been able to properly take note of her, but now that she was better, she was able to see that Carol was more neurotic then she had been at her worst. The temper tantrums and inability to know her own mind were unsettling signs of deep-rooted neurosis. What would happen when Carol discovered that Ayler was an impostor —worse than that—that he was probably the notorious Quentin?

The day seemed to pass at a snail's pace. The drizzle and fog continued. Diana went down to the library for some books and on her way back encountered Paul Miles in the shadowy hallway. He was drugged and moving very slowly, staring straight ahead like a sleepwalker. She halted and drew close to the wall. He passed in the near darkness without seeming to have seen her at all. As she went on to the stairway she realized she was trembling a little. It had been a frightening moment.

She was reading by the window of her room when she heard the creaking of a floorboard behind her. She turned to see that it was Dawn Walsh who had come in so silently. She was startled to see that the former model was wearing a rather elegant black satin dinner dress with a low-cut neck and a full, flowing skirt. The sight of the flowing skirt at once made her think of the phantom she had seen on several occasions. The robe the ghostly creature wore had the same flowing lines as Dawn's dress.

Diana put aside her book and rose to greet her. She said, "You're dressed very elegantly. Is this an important day for you?"

Dawn looked smug. "Don't you like my dress?"

"Very much," she said.

"I'm wearing it so people won't notice my ugliness. I want them to look at the dress instead of my face."

Diana said, "They are bound to notice the dress. But you have no need to be ashamed of your face. You're still beautiful."

Reproach darkened her features. "You know better than that!"

"What I say is true. You're lovely."

"You're like Dr. Meyer and the rest. You enjoy lying to me. And I have been your friend. I warned you about the werewolf."

"I remember."

"The doctor came and took you down there to that bad place," the girl said, looking frightened.

"That wasn't your fault."

"No! I didn't want it!" Dawn protested.

"Then you mustn't think about it," was her reply.

"He was angry about my seeing the werewolf!" Dawn repeated, staring at her oddly.

"Yes. That must have been it," Diana said.

"It came loping across the lawn, and then it halted and stared up at my window," the girl went on.

"You're sure you saw it?"

"Oh, yes," she said. "It was large and a yellowish-gray color and it stayed there a long time before it vanished. It's the werewolf they talk about at Collinwood."

"I suppose so," Diana said. She was taking in all the other girl had to say and trying to make up her mind whether Dawn was the mad murderess or not. Certainly the girl was far removed from reality and showing no hint of improvement.

"It's foggy," Dawn said, shifting her gaze to the window. "Maybe the werewolf will come again tonight."

She frowned. "Why do you say that?"

Dawn looked uneasy. "I don't know. I just thought it might."

Staring at her intently, she asked, "Were you fond of Hope Fenway? Did you really like her?"

Dawn at once seemed to become wary. "I don't remember her."

"Of course you do. She was murdered."

The other girl nodded. "The phantom came for her."

"What phantom?" she asked, picking up on this at once.

"You know!"

"Tell me!"

"The same phantom that came for Dr. Decker," the demented girl said. "If you'd watched, you'd have seen her—the Lost Lady of Turnbridge House!"

"You're making all this up," Diana reprimanded.

"No!" Dawn protested. Then a frightened expression came to her lovely face. "You hate me, and you're trying to trap me!"

"I don't hate you," she protested, going a step closer to the girl in the dark satin gown. "I'm only anxious to find out some facts."

"You hate me!" Dawn repeated in panic and turned and rushed out of the room.

Diana stood there staring after her. It had been an unsettling experience, and it left her more than ever convinced that Dawn could be the murderess. There was even a striking resemblance between the slim, former model and the phantom figure she had seen. Brian Dale was probably right. Dawn was the guilty one.

With a sigh she went back to her chair and picked up the book again, but she could not settle down to read. Instead, she moved to the window to stare out at the heavy mist. The strange and tragic events that had plagued their small community were wreathed in mystery just as the thick fog cloaked the old house. How long before the veil would clear away and they would know the truth?

And where did the spurious Dr. Nils Ayler fit in all this? If he was truly Quentin Collins, what was his motive in being back in Collinsport? Or did he need a motive other than the evil that was forever linked with him? This was the day when Dr. Meyer was supposed to have a showdown with him, but there had been no indication of this confrontation having taken place thus far. And Barnabas was unaccountably absent from the scene!

To make it all the more depressing, there had been her latest quarrel with Carol. This once again emphasized what she'd believed from the start, that Carol should never have come to the clinic with her, though she had insisted. Now, after causing all the trouble with Graham Weeds, she was turning to the impostor who claimed he was Dr. Nils Ayler. For the first time Diana was aware that her sister was not the level-headed, cold person she pretended. Carol was clearly a neurotic!

She had an overwhelming feeling of despair. She didn't want to be alone, yet she could not turn to her sister. It might only mean another quarrel if she went to Carol's room. She didn't know where to find Barnabas either.

Her reverie was broken by a knock on her door. It came so unexpectedly it made her wheel around with a look of fear on her pretty face. Then she had a second and more comforting thought. It could be Barnabas. She hurried over to the door and opened it expectantly.

Her high hopes were doomed. Instead of Barnabas, it was a frowning Dr. Nils Ayler who stood there—and his eyes fixed on her with burning hatred.

CHAPTER TWELVE

"What is it?" she asked nervously.

"Dr. Meyer wants to see you." His tone was heavy with disdain.

"Now?"

"Yes."

"I'll be right down, then," she said, lowering her eyes to avoid the cruel face.

"I'll tell him," he said in his mocking fashion, and walked away swiftly and went down the stairs.

Diana went to her dresser mirror and tidied up her hair a little. She saw that she looked white and shaken, and she worried about what the doctor might want to see her about. After a moment she left the room and went down to his office.

He was apparently waiting for her. As soon as she arrived, he closed the door of the office for privacy and then turned to her anxiously, "Have you any idea where Barnabas is?"

"No," she said, with a frown. "I haven't seen him all day."

"He hasn't been here all day." The doctor sounded worried. "I urgently want to talk to him. I thought since you two are such good friends, he might have confided in you as to where he was going."

"He didn't tell me anything," she said.

"Most unfortunate. I have a certain unpleasant matter to take up with Dr. Ayler, and I'd prefer that Barnabas be here when I undertake it."

"Perhaps he'll return for dinner," she suggested.

"I surely hope he does," Dr. Meyer said. And now he gave her a sharp scanning. "You're not looking so well today. You seem much too tense. Take your tablets. We can't have you suffering from those blackouts again."

"I'll take them," she promised.

Dr. Meyer looked bleak. "The work of the clinic has been badly disrupted, I'm afraid. Perhaps in a few days we can get back to a normal routine once more."

He dismissed her with the manner of one who had lost his ability to make decisions. She knew that he was badly upset. Apparently he didn't want to confront Dr. Ayler until Barnabas was there to back him up in his accusations.

Dinner time arrived, and still there was no sign of Barnabas. The brooding atmosphere of the old house became more overwhelming. Little was said at the dinner table, and afterwards Diana went directly up to her room. She read until her eyes became tired. Then she placed the chair by the door as Barnabas had instructed her and prepared for bed.

It was around ten o'clock when she slipped between the sheets. The weather outside had not improved, and it seemed the others in the old house, as dejected as herself, had all gone to bed early, since the ancient building was mantled with silence. She snapped off her bedside lamp and pulled the covers tightly around her. There wasn't much heat in the room, and the dampness had made it uncomfortable.

Staring up into the shadows she tried to settle her thoughts so sleep would come, but she continued to worry about Barnabas and the strange talk she'd had with the demented Dawn Walsh. She finally dozed off, but it was only to come awake with a start. Sitting up in bed, she tried to decide what had wakened her, and then she seemed to have a vague recollection of the chair by the door being overturned. That was the sound that had intruded on her sleep!

She wanted to reach out and switch on her bedside lamp, but she was too terrified to move. All she could do was strain to penetrate the blackness of the room.

Her heart was pounding, and that throb had come back in her head. She remembered that she'd ignored the doctor's advice to take some of her tablets. Now she deeply regretted it, but it was too late. If she were about to succumb to strain and have another of her blackout spells, there was nothing to be done about it.

From near the foot of her bed she heard a rustle of movement. Trembling seized her, and the ache in her head became so powerful she found her eyes blurred by it. She fought to keep from fainting as she saw the familiar shadowy form of the phantom gradually take shape and come slowly toward her. She could see only the outline of the ghostly intruder.

A scream was frozen on her lips as she watched the frightening thing draw closer to her. Then she at last broke the paralysis that had come over her. She moved to the other side of the bed and took a stand a short distance from the window. But her head was still muddled from the dreadful ache, and she could only wait there for the apparition to reach her.

The phantom figure of the Lost Lady of Turnbridge came slowly across the room. And then in the confusion of the shadows she was able to clearly make out the wan features of Dawn Walsh. The demented girl's lovely face held an odd, stricken expression, and she approached Diana with outstretched hands. This moment welded all Diana's fears into a certainty that the former model in the guise of the phantom had been the murderess.

She gave a scream of terror and struck out wildly at the model. The pale face of Dawn vanished in the shadows at almost the precise instant that Diana was hit by the blackout. She dropped from the frightening reality of the

146

moment into a comforting hammock of black velvet. And there she remained.

The room was flooded with light so suddenly that it was actually painful to her. She was seated in the easy chair by the window and this rush of lights and confused voices was shattering. She cried out in protest. Dr. Meyer was there, and Carol, along with Barnabas and a dazed-looking Paul Miles. They were all grouped around an outstretched figure on the floor just in front of where she sat. As her mind gradually cleared, she stared down at the figure with horror-stricken eyes and saw that it was Dawn Walsh—Dawn Walsh with a large kitchen knife sunk deeply to the handle in her chest and the roughly lispsticked outline of a Scorpion on her forehead!

"No!" she cried and covered her eyes.

Barnabas was at her side immediately. "Don't lose control," he warned her, his arm around her.

Dr. Meyer was on the other side of her chair. "This is horrible!" he said in a weak voice. "What do you know about this, Miss Collins?"

"Can't you see for yourself? She murdered her!" Carol's voice was shrill and hysterical.

"Stop that!" Barnabas warned her harshly. "We have enough problems here without you adding to them."

Carol looked at him with a dazed expression but retreated into silence. Paul Miles stood there, not seeming to take any of it in, but still attracted by the excitement surrounding the scene.

Dr. Meyer asked Diana sternly, "Did you have one of your blackouts?"

"Yes," she said weakly.

"Tell us what happened as nearly as you can remember," the veteran doctor ordered her.

"I woke up and heard someone in the room. Then I saw the phantom figure I've seen so many times before. I got out of bed, and from the shadows Dawn came toward me. I knew she had been the phantom and the one who'd murdered Hope Fenway. I felt the blackout coming on and fought against it, but it did no good." She began to sob.

"You didn't stab Dawn or try to harm her in any way?" Dr. Meyer demanded.

147

"I can only remember what I told you," she said between sobs.

Barnabas spoke up. "I don't think she's in any state for too much questioning at this time."

Dr. Meyer nodded. "That is true."

At the same instant Nils Ayler appeared in the doorway of the room in his dark dressing gown. His eyes opened wide as he saw the body on the floor.

Dr. Meyer told him brusquely, "There's been another murder. Call the police."

"Very well," he said and vanished.

Barnabas said, "I think we should get Diana down to your office. She should be away from all this. Besides, she requires medication."

"Of course," Dr. Meyer agreed.

Barnabas, who had seemed to take command of the situation, told Carol, "Get Paul Miles back to his room. And you'd better remain in your own room until the police want to question you."

Carol gave a show of defiance. "I'll stay with my sister."

It was Dr. Meyer who spoke up now and said, "I consider it in the best interests of your sister for her to be alone. I'll call on you if you are needed."

The blonde girl stood hesitating for a moment as if she might be going to argue with him. Then it appeared she had changed her mind. Taking Paul Miles by the arm, she quietly said, "You'd better come with me."

The stocky architect gave her a dazed look and very obediently went along with her. Diana was beginning to regain some control of herself, and she carefully averted her eyes from the body on the floor.

Barnabas said, "I'll help you down to the doctor's office."

Dr. Meyer took a deep breath. "Do that. I'll be right along. I'll have Dr. Ayler or one of the nurses remain here with this poor girl's body."

Barnabas gave him a warning glance. "You had better make it one of the nurses, considering what we already know about Ayler."

Dr. Meyer looked embarrassed. "Of course, you're right," he murmured.

Diana allowed Barnabas to help her from the chair, and then she put on her dressing gown and slippers. With his aid she left the room. As they went down the hallway they could hear Dr. Ayler talking to the police on the phone. He appeared to be having difficulty making them understand there had been another murder.

The door of Dr. Meyer's office was open, and Barnabas led her inside and saw that she was safely seated in a large leather chair. Then he sat opposite her. There was a troubled expression on his handsome face.

"Is there anything else you can remember?" he asked her.

She shook her head. "No."

"You have no recollection of getting the knife and striking Dawn with it?"

"I can't remember anything about it at all," she said. "From the moment I blacked out until I came to, with you all around me, it's a blank."

Barnabas looked grim. "The police are going to assume you killed Dawn."

"Carol seems to think so."

"I don't care what Carol thinks," he said angrily. "I know better. You're not capable of that kind of cold-blooded murder."

She gave him a despairing look. "How can you be sure I'm not? I may be a different person during these memory lapses."

"I doubt it," Barnabas said.

"Dawn is dead. She was in my room, and I was with her. There has to be some explanation. The easiest one is that I killed her just as I killed Hope Fenway."

"You certainly didn't shove Dr. Decker to his death. You said the phantom did that," he reminded her.

She shrugged. "Maybe I was the phantom. I may have imagined the rest."

"Nor did you try to poison Brian and make it seem a suicide attempt."

"The substitution of stronger pills may have been a genuine accident on the dispensing nurse's part."

"Too pat," he said, rising impatiently and striding back and forth. "In some way all these things are connected. If we had the link, we'd know the whole story."

"I'm sorry, Barnabas," she said sadly. "I think I've failed you. I'm mad and I killed them."

He looked at her angrily. "I don't want to hear such talk from you. That's what they want you to say and think. And it isn't true!"

Nils Ayler came into the room with a nasty look on his arrogant face. "You're talking like a full-fledged psychiatrist, Collins," he snapped in his disdainful fashion. "Do you have a doctor's degree?"

Barnabas looked at him sternly. "I'm probably as qualified as you!"

Ayler flinched for just a second, then said, "Being a mental patient hardly makes you a mental doctor, Mr. Collins!"

The argument might have built between them had not Dr. Meyer arrived. He halted and told his associate, "Keep an eye on the rest of the house, Ayler. Brian Dale is making a fuss and wants to come down here. Tell him he can't. And see that Paul Miles and Miss Collins are all right."

"I will," Ayler promised.

"How soon did the police say they'd be here?" Dr. Meyer wanted to know.

"As soon as they can," Ayler said. "They didn't seem anxious to drive here from Ellsworth so late."

"I'm sorry we couldn't have arranged the murder at a more convenient hour," Meyer said bitingly. "Be on the lookout for them, and close the door after you when you leave."

"Yes, sir," Ayler said as he went out.

Barnabas asked the doctor, "Have you told him yet?"

"No, but I will," Meyer promised.

"You'd better, before the police arrive here," Barnabas warned. "So he'll know where he stands."

The head doctor looked grim. "Yes. I'd been waiting for your return."

"There was no need," Barnabas said.

"I felt it would be better," Dr. Meyer told him.

Then the gray-haired medical man busied himself preparing a glass of some greenish medicine for Diana. He brought it to her and said, "Drink it down. You'll find it bitter but helpful."

She began to sip the vile-tasting potion, fearing she might be ill, as Barnabas and the doctor talked in a low confidential tone at the other side of the room. She wasn't able to hear what they were saying and at this point didn't much care. By the time she finished the glass of green medicine, her head had cleared and she felt much better. But with clarity came the frightening realization of her plight.

Dr. Meyer came back across the room to her. "Did that help?"

"Yes." She gave him the empty glass.

"I want you to do exactly as I tell you," he went on. "I have no desire to see you arrested until I'm positive you killed Dawn Walsh."

"How can I know?"

Dr. Meyer said, "I feel that as we place the evidence together the facts will come out, so you mustn't be too hasty to confess. I'll explain to the police about your blackouts and that you're oblivious to what is going on around you during them."

There was a knock on the door, and Nils Ayler said, "The police are arriving."

"I'll be right there." Dr. Meyer turned to Barnabas, "You remain here with her until I get back."

Barnabas came over beside her, a picture of confidence in his caped coat. Touching a hand to her shoulder, he said, "You must keep calm. Don't rush into anything."

She leaned her cheek against his hand. "Oh, Barnabas! I'm afraid this time it's really bad."

"Don't despair," was his cryptic comment.

They waited. Eventually Dr. Meyer returned with the Inspector. The police officer looked down at her wearily. "I have some questions to ask you," he told her.

"Very well," she said quietly.

She replied to all the questions already put to her by Dr. Meyer and Barnabas. The Inspector wrote her replies down with a bored expression on his weathered face. She guessed that he saw the case as a simple enough one. Dr. Meyer had been unfortunate enough to have one mad girl murder another.

When he'd finished with the questions, the Inspector said, "Dr. Meyer has agreed to be responsible for you, so

I'm going to let you remain here for the night. Make no attempt to leave, do you understand that?"

"Yes," she said weakly.

"There will be officers posted on the grounds, and one man inside the house," the Inspector went on. "Tomorrow we'll begin a full-scale investigation of what has been going on here. I can't promise whether you'll be allowed to remain here then or not."

Dr. Meyer spoke up, "I see no need to worry the girl about that part of it, Inspector."

"Perhaps not. In any case, I'll be wanting to talk to you again in the morning, Miss Collins." He left the office accompanied by Dr. Meyer.

Barnabas waited until they were gone to say, "It wasn't too bad."

"He thinks I killed her."

Barnabas continued to look confident. "We expected that," he told her. "There will be plenty of opportunity to prove otherwise."

She looked down. "They'll dig back in my past and find out I stabbed Graham Weeds. Carol will tell them. They'll link that with the other murders."

He patted her shoulder gently. "Don't think about it."

The office door opened, and Dr. Meyer came back inside. He said, "I've asked Dr. Ayler and your sister to join us here. I have some things to tell the doctor that I think your sister should hear."

Diana gave him a troubled look. "I don't understand."

"You will," Dr. Meyer said, moving behind his desk.

Carol came first and carefully avoided looking at her. She took a position before Dr. Meyer's desk and asked, "Why have you asked me down here? Diana is guilty. I don't want to talk about it. I'll tell my story to the police tomorrow."

Dr. Meyer said, "I don't wish to talk about Diana with you. There's someone else to discuss."

At this point Dr. Ayler came in. He glanced at them all rather uneasily. Then he said, "What is it now?"

Dr. Meyer was looking at Ayler sternly as he told him, "The game is up. I've definite proof you're not Nils Ayler or even a doctor. We've finally identified you, Quentin Collins!"

Carol had been watching the cruel-faced young man. "No!" she cried. "It isn't so! You're not Quentin!"

The shaven-headed man had backed to the door, and there was a mean-looking small gun in his hand. "All right," he said viciously, "so I'm Quentin. It's not going to do you any good! I'll shoot the first one who tries to follow me."

Carol sobbed out, "I don't care whether you're Quentin or not, take me with you!"

He laughed harshly. "You crazy little fool! Why should I want anything to do with a parcel of trouble like you! Tell them about the phantom lady!" he taunted, and with a final mocking laugh he backed out the door.

They all stood transfixed for a moment, paralyzed by the swift change of events. Then Carol let out a sob and rushed out the door after Quentin Collins.

Dr. Meyer raised a warning hand to the others. "Let them go," he said. "There are police out there to look after them!"

Barnabas had moved to the window and drawn back the drapes. "Look!" he cried, pointing out into the darkness.

Diana rushed to his side at the window and peered out into the shadowed night. She was in time to see Quentin Collins fleeing toward a clump of brush at the far left of the mansion. As he vanished, her sister came into sight following after him. But in the next instant a completely unexpected thing happened. From the bushes there emerged a snarling wolf-like creature which sprang in front of Carol, forcing her to halt. A moment later, the police came into the picture, and shots blazed out in the darkness as they fired at the weird animal.

It disappeared as quickly as it had shown itself, and one of the policemen picked up Carol and began carrying her back to the house in his arms. The whole series of incidents had only taken a matter of seconds.

Barnabas gave Diana a strange look. "I think one of the police bullets hit Carol," he said.

This was a signal for them all to rush from the office. They were in the reception hall when the policeman carried Carol in. He took her to a chaise longue in the living room, and Dr. Meyer quickly began to examine

153

her. He raised his eyes to them, and his look left no doubt that she was gravely wounded. Blood was welling from her side.

"It's very bad," he said.

The State Trooper looked despairing. "I didn't intend to hit her. She came across the path of the bullet just as I fired."

Dr. Meyer was already giving Barnabas instructions as to what he needed, and a nurse appeared to help him. Barnabas carried the wounded girl to the operating table in the examining room, and Dr. Meyer shortly began an emergency operation to retrieve the bullet and try to save her life. The vigil began outside the examining room. Diana was too stunned to have any idea of the passing time.

At last Dr. Meyer came out to them. "She's dying," he said. "But she wants to talk to you, Diana." He gave Barnabas a significant glance. "I'd say one of the police officers should be in the room to hear what she says, as well. We'll have to be very quiet. She's terribly weak now and can only speak in a whisper."

Carol was in the bed in the room next to the examining room. The light in the room was soft, but it was easy to see death already starkly written on her pale face. As they assembled by her bedside, Dr. Meyer leaned close to her and quietly told her, "Diana is here."

Carol's eyelids flicked open, and she stared up at Diana. With great strain and in a hoarse whisper she said, "I killed Dawn . . . I was the one. Killed Hope, as well. And Dr. Decker. Wanted it blamed on you!"

"You mustn't say such things," Diana begged, her eyes filling with tears.

"I was the phantom lady. Came with you to get you in bad trouble. Graham made me do it. He was no truer to me than Quentin. Bad luck with men! After Graham left you, he pretended to love me. A lie! He's deep in debt to the estate. Played game to keep me quiet. When I found out, I stabbed him. You found him with knife in him and blacked out. He promised not to incriminate me if I got rid of you. So I came here and fell in love with Quentin!" She broke off and seemed to be choking.

Diana turned to Dr. Meyer. "Do something for her!"

154

The doctor bent over the dying girl and held a handkerchief saturated with something to her nostrils. The choking spell eased off. Then Carol signaled that she wanted to speak with Diana again. Her voice weaker than before, she said, "Quentin helped me. But didn't tell me who he was. Tricked me just like Graham. We changed tablets on Brian because we thought he suspected us. I wanted you to think you were the killer and be placed in an asylum or have you kill yourself. It didn't work out. I'm the unlucky sister!" The choking came again, and this time it ended only as she breathed her last.

Barnabas took the shocked Diana from the room. "At least she lived to tell the truth and absolve you of any guilt," he said. "I suspected her from the start, but then I became confused by other things."

Dr. Meyer gave her a strong sleep potion. She didn't awake until noon. By that time the sun had returned. It was a fine autumn day, and Brian Dale was seated by her bed. The young playwright had apparently fully recovered, for he was dressed and seemed as healthy as ever.

He gave her a sympathetic look. "You had a long sleep," he said.

She sat up. "Yes. I needed it."

"It's going to be all right," he told her. "I'll get one of the nurses to help you."

"I don't really need her," she protested.

"Better to be safe," he said, rising. "I've just been sitting here doing the bedside watch bit."

She said, "Thank you, Brian." And then, "It wasn't all a dreadful nightmare, was it?"

He looked down at her soberly. "No, it wasn't," he said.

She nodded, and he went out. She'd known it had been real, but yet it was almost too harrowing to believe. Carol a murderess and dead! How her sister must have hated her! And what a weak, unfortunate person Carol had been. First turned to a path of crime by Graham Weeds, and then by Quentin Collins. Quentin had undoubtedly made his escape, as he had so many times before. But Graham could be made to pay for his evil.

The moment she went downstairs she inquired about Barnabas from Dr. Meyer. "I want to talk to him," she said.

The senior doctor looked embarrassed. "He has gone," he said.

"Gone?" she echoed.

"Yes. He's finished with his treatments here. I couldn't ask him to remain any longer. He spoke of going to the old house at Collinwood and preparing for a journey somewhere."

Her pretty face was filled with despair. "But he can't leave that way! I have to see him!" She turned to the doctor again. "Can Brian Dale drive me over there?"

"If you like," the doctor said. "Both you and he are ready to be discharged. There's no reason why you shouldn't have freedom to go and come as you please."

Brian at the wheel of the station wagon lost no time in getting to the old house. He seemed unhappy about her mission but still anxious to help, and she felt a pang of sympathy for the likable young man who she knew was in love with her. When he brought the car to a halt in front of the old house, he helped her out and was ready to go inside with her.

Turning to him she said, "No, Brian. I must go in alone."

He looked hurt. "Will you be all right?"

"Yes."

"I'll wait," he said. "I'll wait in the station wagon."

"You needn't," she warned him, her eyes gentle.

He was quietly determined. "I will, just the same."

So she left him standing there and went up the steps and knocked on the door. A moment later the unkempt Hare let her in. He glowered at her, but allowed her to make her way to the living room. There was no sign of Barnabas there. She tried a couple of the other rooms without success, either. Then she saw Hare standing watching her.

"Where is he?" she demanded.

The mute servant pointed downward, indicating the cellar.

A shadow of fear came to her, and she hesitated. But then she conquered the uneasiness and walked through the shadows to the cellar steps. She made her way down to the earthen floor, and from there she could see a faint glow of light from the doorway of the hidden room.

Resolutely she made her way along the length of the dark cellar until she came to the open door. She entered the dimly lighted room, but Barnabas was not there! And then she heard her name softly whispered. A look of terror crossed her face! The whisper had come from the casket in the far corner.

Her love for Barnabas overcame all terror, and she advanced to the side of the casket. He lay there, his handsome face relaxed, his hands folded.

He had returned to the world of the dead!

"Barnabas!" she cried unhappily.

Then a miracle took place. He opened his eyes, smiled at her sadly, and raised himself out of the coffin. "Resurrections are few and far between," he told her. "And mine, I'm afraid, is a fake one. I heard you come down the cellar stairs, and I decided to let you know what I have been through. To give you a hint of the horror of it."

She looked at him earnestly. "But that's over. You're cured!"

The handsome Britisher swung out of the coffin and stood beside her. "I hope that is true. But I may never be sure." His voice became gentle. "So for your sake, little Diana, it has to be goodbye."

"No," she protested, clinging to him.

His arms were around her. "Who brought you here?"

"Brian," she said. "He's up there waiting. I told him not to, but he insisted."

"What a fine, wise young man he is," Barnabas said. He kissed her gently on the lips. "Go to him. He needs you. You need each other."

"I can't leave you now," she protested.

"Go," he said gently, but with great authority, and she obeyed him. She started down the dark length of the cellar and turned back only once. He was standing by the casket. They waved goodbye, and it was over.

You Will Also Want To Read ...

BARNABAS, QUENTIN AND THE NIGHTMARE ASSASSIN
by Marilyn Ross
Quentin tries to escape death at the hands of a killer he himself has hired.
(63-363, 60¢)

BARNABAS, QUENTIN AND THE CRYSTAL COFFIN
by Marilyn Ross
Barnabas and Quentin clash when a young heiress tries to solve the mystery of her twin sister's death.
(63-385, 60¢)

BARNABAS, QUENTIN AND THE WITCH'S CURSE
by Marilyn Ross
Will Barnabas be able to prevent Quentin from establishing his coven of witches at Collinwood?
(63-402, 60¢)

BARNABAS, QUENTIN AND THE HAUNTED CAVE
by Marilyn Ross
Barnabas is hunted by a phantom killer in the domain of the dead.
(63-427, 60¢)

BARNABAS, QUENTIN AND THE FRIGHTENED BRIDE
by Marilyn Ross
Barnabas clashes with a mysterious masked stranger in an effort to save the life of a beautiful bride.
(63-446, 60¢)

THE DARK SHADOWS BOOK
OF VAMPIRES AND WEREWOLVES

Horror Tales Selected By
Barnabas and Quentin Collins
of ABC-TV's Hit Show
Dark Shadows

"Rarely is the ordinary mortal granted an opportunity to know the torment and suffering that is the lot of the vampire or the werewolf. Objects of disgust, horror, and fear, we are hunted down like the lowliest of beasts and hounded to a destruction far more degrading than that affored common criminals, for the curse that makes us what we are also makes men forget that once we were as they are—happy creatures permitted the joys of sunlight, and flowers, and the simplest pleasures of life.

"Here, then, is a singular collection of tales and narratives gleaned from the shelves of fiction and fact, offering readers a glimpse of the truth as it really is."

—*From the Introduction by Barnabas
and Quentin Collins*

(63-419, 60c)